A.D. STARRLING

A WITCH QUEEN NOVELLA

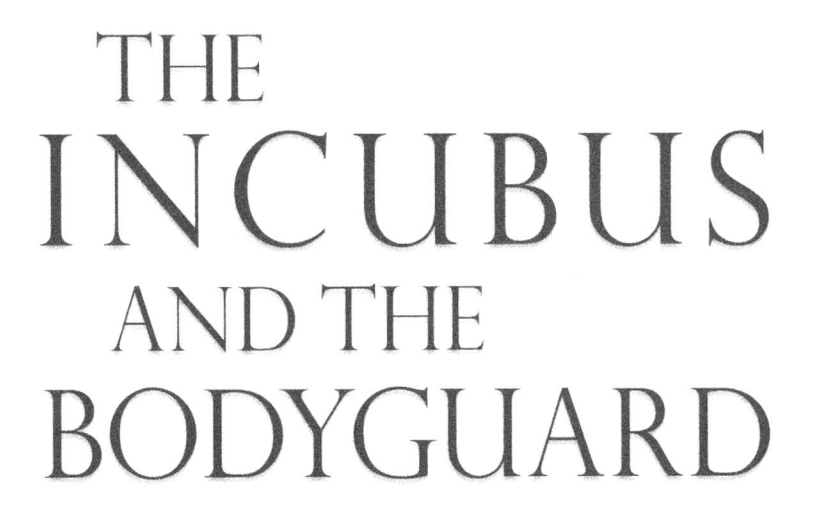

THE INCUBUS AND THE BODYGUARD

COPYRIGHT

The Incubus and The Bodyguard
(A Witch Queen Novella)
Copyright © AD Starrling 2024. All rights reserved. Registered with the US Copyright Service.
Hardback edition
ISBN: 978-1-912834-52-5

www.ADStarrling.com
shop.adstarrling.com

Edited by The Wallflower Editing

The right of AD Starrling to be identified as the author of this work has been asserted in accordance with the Copyright, Designs and Patents Act 1988. All rights reserved. No parts of this book may be reproduced in any form or by any electronic or mechanical means, including information storage and retrieval systems, without the prior written consent of the author, excepting for brief quotes used in reviews. Your respect of the author's rights and hard work is appreciated. Request to publish extracts from this book should be sent to the author at ads@adstarrling.com. This book is a work of fiction. References to real people (living or dead), events, establishments, organizations, or locations are intended only to provide a sense of authenticity, and are used factitiously. All other characters, and all other incidents and dialogue, are drawn from the author's imagination and are not to be construed as real.

BOOKS BY A.D. STARRLING

Seventeen Novels

Hunted

Warrior

Empire

Legacy

Origins

Destiny

Seventeen Short Stories

First Death

Dancing Blades

The Meeting

The Warrior Monk

The Hunger

The Bank Job

Legion

Blood and Bones

Fire and Earth

Awakening

Forsaken

Hallowed Ground

Heir

Legion

Witch Queen
The Darkest Night
Rites of Passage
Of Flames and Crows
Midnight Witch
A Fury of Shadows
Witch Queen
The Incubus and The Bodyguard

Seventeen Universe
The Party

Division Eight
Mission:Black
Mission: Armor
Mission:Anaconda

Miscellaneous
Void - A Sci-fi Horror Short Story
The Other Side of the Wall - A Horror Short Story

CHAPTER ONE

The gleam of the gold leaf adorning the walls and columns of *Oro Divino* made Vlad Vissarion's eyes hurt when he walked inside the high-end Italian restaurant on the Upper East Side. It didn't help that he was still recovering from a hangover, one of several he'd suffered this past month.

The way his familiar Tarang flicked his tail beside him indicated the tiger was still annoyed by his recent behavior.

"Mr. Vissarion." The maitre d'hotel left his post and came to greet him, his expression slightly nervous.

Vlad dipped his head. "Antonio. Is everything ready?"

"Yes, sir. Follow me."

Though the man couldn't see Tarang, he naturally avoided the space where the tiger walked. Familiars were only visible to those who possessed magic in their soul or if they wished to make their presence known.

Vlad could feel dozens of eyes on him as he crossed the

main restaurant area. It wasn't just his looks that made him the center of attention when he entered a room. His incubus powers played a part in it too.

They took the elevator to the third floor of the converted nineteenth-century brownstone. Antonio led him down a corridor to a sumptuous private dining room.

Vlad slowed to a stop, his gaze sweeping the space where two of New York's most notorious crime families would soon attempt to broker a peace deal.

It offered a commanding view of Madison Avenue through its floor-to-ceiling windows. One he would normally have found pleasing were it not for the company he would soon be keeping.

The *Black Devils* men stationed discreetly around the room greeted him with silent nods.

A dull headache hammered at Vlad's temples. He swallowed a sigh.

I'd rather be spending my Friday night at home than deal with the inevitable drama this evening will bring. His chest tightened. *Then again, the place feels too empty now that Mae is gone.*

Mae Jin, the Witch Queen of prophecy, had been temporarily staying at his apartment in Chelsea until she finally defeated the Sorcerer King, who had long ruled the world of magic. Though it had been four months since the battle on Brooklyn Bridge that had sealed the fate of all witches and sorcerers in the world, the encounter remained harrowingly fresh in Vlad's mind. Not least because he'd finally met his father Ilmon, the king of Incubi and Succubi, and learned the truth about his birth.

Tarang bumped the back of his hand with his nose.

Vlad looked into the tiger's limpid blue eyes. *Are you trying to comfort me?*

Tarang huffed, the bond that connected them singing warmly between their souls. Though Vlad could not hear his familiar's thoughts like Mae could hers, he was acutely aware of the tiger's emotions.

He perused the guy behind the bar and the uniformed figures setting the dining table dominating the space.

"The staff knows what to do in case this shit goes south, right?"

Antonio paled a little. "*Will* it go south, sir?"

Vlad shrugged. "This is the Italians we're talking about. They're not exactly known for their sangfroid."

The maitre d'hotel swallowed. "I shall keep that in mind, sir. And yes, they know the drill. Keep low, get out, and pretend to be dumb about the whole thing if they're questioned by the police."

The *Oro Divino* belonged to the *Black Devils*. Everyone who worked there had signed a confidentiality agreement to keep their mouths shut about what they saw and heard on the premises. The pay more than made up for the inconvenience. Plus, many of the staff had fled other criminal gangs and benefited from the protection of the ruling New York *Bratva*.

A bout of sympathy danced through Vlad at Antonio's worried expression. He patted the man's shoulder.

"There'll be a special tip for everyone if this dinner concludes without bloodshed."

A flush of color flooded the maitre d'hotel's cheeks.

Vlad dialed down his incubus charms. His cellphone rang just as the man left.

He moved to the windows overlooking Madison Avenue and took the call.

"How's it going?" Yuliy Vissarion said without preamble.

"It hasn't started yet."

There was a short silence. "Let's hope this goes off without a hitch," the head of the *Black Devils* said in a tired voice. "We have a lot riding on it."

Vlad frowned. He could imagine his uncle smoking one of the cigars he liked so much behind the white granite desk in his modern study, in the fifteen-thousand-square-foot Brooklyn mansion he called his home.

"You know, I'm not sure I'm enjoying the new role our overlords in Moscow decided to bestow upon us," the incubus said coolly. "None of our men signed up for this gig to be peacemakers of the criminal underworld."

"Be that as it may, we can't be seen to fail," Yuliy grunted. "Our reputation will suffer a huge blow if this peace deal falls through."

Vlad ran a hand irritably through his hair.

He supposed he should be grateful his uncle had sent him to mediate the negotiations between the Lucianos and the *Red Dragon* Triad rather than make him sit through another lecture about his duties as the heir to their group.

A familiar figure appeared in the dining room doorway.

Vlad stared.

"By the way, I forgot to mention something," Yuliy said. "Someone will be acting as an external observer for these negotiations. Call it backup in case things go wrong and we get blamed for it."

"Would this someone be a former member of the *Bacatá Cartel* by any chance?" Vlad asked with a sigh.

"How'd you know?" Yuliy said without compunction.

"I'm looking at him."

Vlad ended the call and watched the man coming toward him.

"Really, an external observer?" he asked Enrique Cortes drily. He grabbed the Colombian's hand and pulled him into a quick bear hug.

"What can I say?" Cortes smiled. "I'm apparently a popular peacekeeper in the criminal underworld."

Vlad grimaced. They both knew Cortes used to be one of the most ruthless mobsters in South America before his core was repaired by Mae a few months back and he officially returned to the world of magic as the head of the Medellin coven.

The Colombian sorcerer's familiar hopped down from his shoulder and landed lightly on Tarang's head.

"How're you doing there, tiger?" Popo said brightly.

Tarang huffed testily at the red Macaw.

"Did someone forget to take his happy pills this morning?" Popo asked with undeterred cheerfulness.

Vlad arched an eyebrow. "Why is he so peppy?"

"I may have promised to take him on a date to his favorite place in the city tomorrow," Cortes replied with a long-suffering sigh.

"And where's that, exactly?" Vlad said warily.

"The zoo." Cortes shrugged at Vlad's expression. "I

don't get it either. You'd think it'd be the last place he'd want to go, what with being in a cage most of his life."

"Your parrot is weird."

"I have the same thought every single day," Cortes muttered.

A waiter brought them drinks.

Vlad took the glass of champagne and looked out over Madison Avenue.

"Have you heard from Mae?" Cortes asked, his gaze on the bright lights outside.

Vlad wasn't fooled by his neutral tone.

"Not since she and Nikolai left for Europe," he replied in a level voice.

Cortes hesitated. "Anya got a message from Mae yesterday."

Anya Mendes was the daughter of the High Priest of the Rio de Janeiro coven. A powerful witch with the unique ability to cast Illusion Sorcery, she and Cortes were now officially engaged.

"Oh yeah?" Vlad said with studied indifference.

"Mae and Nikolai are planning to get a place together in Brooklyn when they get back."

A hot feeling stabbed through Vlad's heart at Cortes's words.

"Are they now?" He picked an imaginary piece of lint off his Armani suit.

Tarang made a soft sound and rubbed against his leg.

"Yes." Cortes wrinkled his brow, evidently not buying the act either. "You need to put her behind you. Nothing will come from moping after Mae."

"I'm not moping," Vlad denied.

Cortes raised an eyebrow.

"It's been four months," Vlad said a tad sullenly. "I'm allowed to mope a little still. I did love her after all."

Cortes watched him carefully over the rim of his champagne flute.

"You slept with anyone recently?"

Vlad narrowed his eyes. Anyone else asking that question would have been looking for their teeth next.

"Why, are you offering your services?" he grunted.

Cortes made a face. "You and I both know our dicks would shrivel up and die if we saw each other naked."

Popo straightened on Tarang's head, his golden eyes gleaming. "My Enrique, you must keep your options open. You never know what might happen in the—*mmph*! *Mmph!*"

Cortes had muzzled the parrot.

Vlad grimaced. "Is everything okay between you and Anya?"

"It's peachy, thank you." Cortes gave Popo a dark look.

"By the way, why are you still representing the *Bacatá Cartel*?"

"Are you trying to change the subject?"

"Yes and no." Vlad eyed the Colombian curiously. "I thought you cut all ties with your old family."

"I did." Cortes rubbed the back of his neck awkwardly. "My old boss asked me for a favor. To be fair, I owed him one."

Vlad gave him a puzzled look.

"Remember when Anya and I got attacked by those hellbeasts after we left the cartel compound?" Cortes said.

"Well, they ended up having to deal with them. They lost a few good men that day."

Vlad frowned. The attack had been orchestrated by the Sorcerer King in an attempt to get his hands on Cortes's rare Arcane Magic.

"Boss."

Vlad turned. Ilya had appeared in the doorway. His oldest serving bodyguard was dressed in an immaculate black suit that hid the gun under his left armpit, his face set in the stony expression that was his calling card. Milo, Vlad's second bodyguard, appeared behind Ilya.

"They're here," Ilya said tersely.

A buzz of tension coursed through Vlad. He focused on the reason they were there tonight.

"Show them in."

CHAPTER TWO

Giovanni Luciano entered first. The don of the Italian crime family was accompanied by his youngest son, Marco, and flanked by four men who moved with the deadly grace of trained killers. Though in his late sixties, Giovanni still cut an imposing figure, his silver hair swept back from an austere face that had graced the cover of *Time* magazine twice.

Behind him came Wei Chen, her designer dress emphasizing a figure that belied her seventy years. The leader of the *Red Dragon* Triad had taken over her husband's empire after his death a decade ago and turned it into one of the most powerful criminal organizations in Asia and the United States.

She was escorted by her son James and a couple of bodyguards who looked like they could snap a person in half without breaking a sweat.

"Welcome to *Oro Divino*." Vlad put his glass on a side

table and strolled across the room, a charming smile stretching his mouth. "I trust you had a pleasant journey?"

Giovanni grunted a greeting. Wei Chen's ruby-painted lips curved.

"Always a pleasure, Vlad," she purred.

Her gaze swept over him appreciatively, lingering on his broad shoulders and his chest.

Vlad's smile didn't falter.

It wasn't the first time Wei Chen had attempted to hit on him. He'd learned early on in his dealings with her that it was all a carefully crafted act, designed to make people underestimate her razor-sharp mind.

"Please." He indicated the dining table. "Make yourselves comfortable."

The crime bosses and their sons took seats opposite one another, their retinues standing to attention to the side. Ilya and Milo positioned themselves near the door, hands clasped loosely in front of them.

Cortes strolled to an armchair by the window, seemingly absorbed in his phone. Popo preened his feathers nonchalantly on the Colombian's shoulder.

Vlad knew better. Both the sorcerer and his familiar would unleash mayhem at a moment's notice.

James Chen observed Cortes with a pinched expression. "What's he doing here?"

Marco Luciano was similarly eyeing the Colombian like he was a piece of trash stuck to the bottom of his designer shoe.

Vlad dimly recalled there was no love lost between the three men.

"Our *Bratva* appointed him as an external observer."

Though he kept his tone light, Wei Chen's and Giovanni's expressions cooled at his hidden warning.

At least now everyone knows where they stand.

A low rumble had him looking down. Tarang stood stone-still beside him. He was staring at something Vlad couldn't see, his pupils gleaming with a faint trace of crimson magic.

Vlad's scalp prickled. He focused on his familiar's bond and picked up on the unease thrumming through it.

Tarang blinked, sudden confusion flowing across their connection. He unfroze, his tail swaying anxiously.

Vlad scanned the room. He couldn't sense anything out of the ordinary.

Giovanni made an impatient sound.

Vlad masked his disquiet and settled into the chair at the head of the table.

The staff began serving the food.

"Shall we begin?" Vlad said as they finished their entrées. "I believe we're here to discuss the matter of the Brooklyn docks."

Giovanni's weathered face hardened. "Those docks have belonged to my family for three generations." He stabbed his mullet fillet sautéed in sea snail sauce, his gimlet eyes on Wei Chen.

"Yet your men killed two of my people there last week," the Triad leader said silkily. She cut delicately into a seared duck breast served with passion fruit, endive, and a parfait of livers.

"They were trespassing on private property," Giovanni grunted.

"Since when is murder the answer to trespassing?" Wei Chen countered.

Giovanni's eyes shrank to slits. He pointed his fork at the Triad leader.

"So, you admit they were trespassing?"

Vlad swallowed a sigh and took a sip of his water.

Maybe I should have ordered whiskey.

Tarang issued a berating huff where he'd plopped on the floor next to his chair.

Wei Chen put her cutlery down and dabbed daintily at her mouth with her linen napkin. "That's not what I said, Gio. And I would appreciate it if your lackey stopped playing with that trigger." Her dark gaze found Marco.

Giovanni's son's hand was on the gun in his shoulder holster.

The Triad bodyguards shifted, their movements so subtle most people would have missed them. James Chen tensed, one hand sliding toward the weapon Vlad knew he carried at his back.

"How about everyone calms down?" Vlad said coldly. "We're here for a negotiation, not a shoot-out."

Giovanni cut his eyes to his son. Marco relented and dropped his hand from his gun. The Italian don's attention returned to his nemesis.

"Your dealers were moving their products through our territory without my family's permission." His voice dropped dangerously. "What did you expect would happen?"

"We had an agreement." Wei Chen's perfectly manicured nails drummed the tablecloth, her face tight. "Or have you conveniently forgotten the arrangement we came to regarding the movement of certain goods through your routes?"

"That agreement was nullified the moment you started dealing with the Jamaicans," Giovanni retorted.

Vlad's pulse quickened. This was the first he was hearing about Caribbean elements getting involved in the New York underworld. Across the room, Cortes had lowered his phone, his expression growing focused.

"The deal my Triad has with certain parties in Kingston is none of your concern, Gio," Wei Chen said curtly. "Besides, nothing is set in stone yet. We are still investigating our potential business partners."

Marco leaned forward, his expensive suit pulling tight across his shoulders. "Be that as it may, it becomes our concern when those parties start moving through our territory without paying their dues."

"You mean the protection money you charge that's three times what we agreed upon?" James snapped.

The temperature in the room dropped several degrees. Vlad could practically taste the animosity crackling between the two heirs.

"Gentlemen." He kept his voice measured and released a faint wave of the incubus charm that had gotten him out of many a tricky situation in the past. "Perhaps we should take a moment to—"

Something strange brushed against his senses, like oil sliding over water. Vlad stiffened.

The sensation made his skin crawl.

Tarang's growl vibrated against his leg. The tiger's alarm flooded their bond as he uncoiled and rose, hackles rising and muscles bunching beneath his gleaming coat.

Cortes straightened across the way. "Do you feel that?"

Popo had stopped preening his feathers and was watching the room with unusual intensity.

Vlad's mouth went dry. "Yes."

The sinister magic dancing across his skin reminded him of the corruption that had emanated from the Sorcerer King during their final battle. But it felt worse, somehow.

Giovanni glanced between Vlad and Cortes, decades of survival instinct clearly warning him something was amiss. "Something the matter?"

"I'm not sure." Vlad forced a smile and pushed away from the table. "Excuse me for a moment."

Wei Chen's shrewd gaze narrowed. She opened her mouth to say something.

The lights went out with a suddenness that made her draw a sharp breath.

CHAPTER THREE

Chairs scraped as everyone shot to their feet. The sound of multiple safeties clicking off sounded eerily loud in the darkness.

Panicked murmurs rose from the staff.

"Nobody move!" Vlad barked.

"What the hell is going on?!" James snarled to his left.

Crimson flared around Vlad as he drew on his incubus powers, the familiar heat of his demon magic settling in his veins and across his bond with Tarang. The darkness retreated slightly, allowing him to make out shapes around the table.

Giovanni and Wei Chen stared nervously at the red light dancing off his body. James and Marco blanched.

They'd heard the rumors about him.

"Is that—?" Wei Chen started.

Cortes's shout had them flinching. *"Shield!"*

The sorcerer was on his feet, his sword and whip in hand. Golden light bloomed around him, his Arcane

Magic casting their shadows across the walls and ceiling. Popo's eyes and wings glowed as the familiar manifested his presence and his powers.

The restaurant staff scrambled backward wildly, their faces white with terror where they'd dropped to the floor. Vlad's men watched the room tensely, weapons in hand.

Marco whipped his gun from his shoulder holster. The muzzle swung wildly between Vlad and Cortes, fear making the whites of his eyes gleam in the gloom.

"Put that down!" Giovanni barked.

Wei Chen was frowning at Cortes.

A flicker of movement caught Vlad's eyes. His heart stuttered.

Dark shapes were dropping into view outside the windows, their forms barely visible against the night sky and the city backdrop. They crashed through the glass in a shower of sparkling shards, the screams of pedestrians drifting up from Madison Avenue drowning out some of the noise as deadly fragments rained down on them.

The masked figures unclipped the ropes they'd rappelled down from their harnesses and raised the automatic firearms hanging from their chests.

"*Get down!*" Vlad roared.

He tackled Wei Chen as bullets started flying. They hit the ground hard.

The crime boss grunted but had the sense to stay still.

Vlad rolled and came up in a crouch in front of her, the diamond studs in his ears shifting to deadly swords as they dropped into his hands. The blades hummed with the same crimson energy that made his eyes and flesh glow, an extension of his demonic heritage.

Crockery crashed as the Triad bodyguards and Giovanni's men flipped the table and dragged their charges behind it. Bullets scored the wood, filling the air with wood chips.

Vlad's heart slammed wildly against his ribs as he glanced over his shoulder.

Thank God I asked Yuliy to bulletproof that thing!

Kevlar gleamed inside the holes cratering the table's surface.

Tarang's snarl filled the air as he launched himself at the nearest attacker.

Marco gurgled. James cursed. The way the Italian and Chinese bodyguards recoiled told Vlad they could see the tiger too.

Giovanni and Wei Chen stared unblinkingly, unable to drag their gazes from the familiar who'd made himself visible so as to engage the enemy.

They'd heard rumors about the tiger too.

Tarang brought down one of the masked figures with devastating force, his fangs tearing the man's jugular open like it was paper, the spray of hot blood painting his muzzle crimson. He batted another man with a powerful strike from his paw that sent him flying into a wall with the sound of breaking bones.

Some dozen more assailants came through the windows, their dark tactical gear absorbing what little light poured in from outside as they fired at the *Black Devils* men trying to get the restaurant staff to safety.

Vlad clenched his jaw. *Someone planned this!*

"Boss!" Milo's shout carried over the chaos.

Vlad's head snapped around. His youngest bodyguard

was trading shots with three masked attackers who had burst through the door, his face tight with concentration where he crouched behind a column.

Ilya grabbed two men running toward Vlad by the back of their heads and smashed their skulls together. He turned and shot another one point-blank in the eye.

The strange magic Vlad had sensed earlier grew stronger, making his stomach roil. Cortes joined him, the Colombian cursing viciously in Spanish as he brought an assailant down with his sword.

"There's something seriously wrong with this magic, whatever the hell it is!" he barked.

The sorcerer's whip cracked through the air and wrapped around another attacker's throat. He yanked viciously. The man's neck snapped with a wet crunch.

"Ilya! Get them out of here!" Vlad jerked his head at Giovanni and Wei Chen where they crouched behind the overturned table, their bodyguards forming a protective circle around them and their sons.

Ilya hesitated before nodding. He herded the crime bosses and their retinues toward the kitchen where the *Black Devils* had evacuated the staff.

A grunt had Vlad's head swinging around.

Milo clutched his bleeding shoulder where he'd been shot, his gun hanging loosely in his limp grip. He clenched his jaw as two men aimed their weapons at him.

Vlad brought the bodyguard's assailants down with the demonic spell he'd learned to cast from his father in Hell, the scarlet energy sphere evaporating flesh and bone as it tore through them and blasted a five-foot-wide hole in the wall.

The remaining men converged on him.

Vlad stood his ground and effortlessly blocked the shots whizzing toward him with his swords, the bullets pinging off the blades and clattering to the floor.

A roar left his throat as he lifted the lid on his powers.

Demonic magic detonated from him on a violent crimson wave that made the chandeliers tremble and his attackers falter. They flinched at the ferocious sound that issued from Tarang, the noise rattling the glass behind the bar.

Vlad and Tarang moved, his swords and his familiar's fangs and claws finding easy targets as they flitted amidst their targets in a macabre dance of death. Cortes's blade gleamed across the way as he opened an attacker from navel to sternum. Popo dive-bombed another man, his wings trailing golden light as he struck the guy in the eyes with his claws.

The hairs lifted on the back of Vlad's neck. He ducked, narrowly missing the saber that would have decapitated him. He dropped and twisted as he kicked out. The masked figure who'd attacked him jumped, avoiding his attempt to swipe his legs out from under him.

Metal whistled close to Vlad's face.

He leaned back sharply and raised his swords in a cross guard. Steel rang against diamond in a shower of sparks.

Vlad clenched his jaw.

This guy is good.

A scream from the direction of the kitchen made his shoulders knot.

He kept his gaze on his attacker and gave Tarang a silent command.

Go!

Tarang hesitated, his worried gaze swinging from Vlad to the lithe man standing a short distance away, the stranger's dark pupils gleaming dangerously above his mask.

I'll be alright. Vlad cut his eyes briefly to the familiar. *Protect our people!*

The tiger whirled around with an irritated sound and bounded for the kitchen.

The masked man resumed his attack, each strike flowing into the next with deadly grace. But Vlad hadn't survived this long in the criminal underworld by being an easy target to bring down.

He feinted left and drove his right blade through his attacker's guard. The man moved to avoid it and stepped right into the path of Vlad's second sword.

Blood sprayed as diamond pierced flesh. His attacker stumbled back, clutching his shoulder.

Vlad was about to deliver the final blow when pain exploded inside his body with a suddenness that made black spots swarm his vision.

He gasped, his swords slipping from suddenly numb fingers. Ice filled his veins, spreading outward from his core on a wave that stole his breath and made his heart stutter.

The sensation was like nothing he'd ever experienced.

It felt as if someone had reached inside him and twisted, corrupting the very essence of what he was.

What's happening to me?!

The sickening gleam Vlad glimpsed in his attacker's eyes before the man retreated into the shadows told him he'd fallen into the enemy's trap.

Tarang's roar of distress echoed through their bond, the tiger's anguish slamming into Vlad like a physical blow as their connection started to fray.

The world tilted sideways.

The last thing Vlad saw before darkness claimed him was Cortes's alarmed expression as the sorcerer bolted toward him, his mouth open on a desperate shout Vlad never heard.

CHAPTER FOUR

The first thing Vlad registered when he came to was a bitter taste in his mouth. The second was the cold ground beneath his back and the shrill wail of sirens.

A warm weight pressed against his flank, taking away some of the chill seeping into his bones. He knew without opening his eyes that it was Tarang.

But the tiger's presence felt odd.

Their bond, usually a vibrant connection singing between their souls, seemed pale and strangely muted.

Someone was talking to him. Vlad forced his eyes open.

Cortes's troubled face swam into view. "Can you hear me?!"

Vlad tried to speak. His throat felt like sandpaper. He settled for a grunt instead.

"Here."

A bottle of water appeared. Cortes helped him sit up

and held it to his lips. Vlad drank greedily, his head pounding.

Popo was perched on Tarang, the familiar crooning softly to the anxious tiger as he hugged Vlad's side.

They were on Madison Avenue. Red and blue lights strobed across the building beside him, casting strange shadows across the glittering facade. A crowd gathered behind the police cordons, their phones held high as they recorded the incident.

Memory returned in violent flashes of color. Vlad's stomach lurched.

He met Cortes's gaze wildly. "The restaurant—!"

"Everyone made it out okay," Cortes reassured him hastily. "Ilya got your staff and guests safely through the back. Your men had already secured the rear alley. A few of them got injured in the gunfight. Nothing that won't heal." He paused. "Marco took a bullet to his shoulder and Ilya one to the thigh. "

Vlad's throat tightened. "Ilya got shot?"

"Yes."

Anger brought a flush of heat to Vlad's clammy face.

"Wei Chen and Giovanni?" he asked Cortes stiffly.

"Still processing what they saw." Cortes grimaced. "Kinda hard not to when a tiger materializes out of thin air and starts tearing people apart."

Tarang huffed softly beside them, his muzzle clean of the blood of their enemies. The familiar's anxiety pulsed weakly through their weakened bond.

Vlad's jaw hardened.

If that's even the right word for what I'm feeling.

He remembered his second bodyguard and looked around. "Milo?"

"Getting patched up in the ambulance." Cortes indicated the vehicle parked at the curb a short distance away. "He's more pissed about his suit getting ruined than the bullet wound." The Colombian's mouth curved wryly. "The paramedics wanted to put you in one to check you over, but I said you'd be better off getting some fresh air out here. Tarang's presence inside an ambulance wouldn't exactly go unnoticed. He hasn't left your side since you passed out."

Vlad reached out and stroked the tiger's neck weakly. Tarang huffed and turned his giant head to lick his hand, his tongue rasping hotly across his palm.

Cortes hesitated. "The men who attacked this place? They vanished the moment you went down. Like they'd pulled off what they came here to do."

Vlad's recollection of the fight was still hazy, but he remembered the masked figure who'd attacked him with a saber. The man's expression before he'd disappeared had been one of triumph.

A wave of dizziness swept over him. He swallowed and closed his eyes.

"Vlad?" Cortes said, alarmed.

The Colombian's voice sounded faint above the roaring in his ears.

Something felt wrong.

Vlad reached instinctively for his incubus powers.

The familiar heat that always simmered beneath his skin and in his blood failed to manifest.

His eyes snapped open. Fear drenched him in a cold sweat.

He pressed a hand to his stomach and tried again. Nothing happened.

"What's wrong?" Cortes was watching him with a heavy scowl.

Footsteps approached before Vlad could reply. They looked around.

Jared Dickson was headed for them. An Immortal tasked with the role of a liaison between the Immortal Societies and the US Special Affairs Bureau, the NYPD Lieutenant had been a crucial figure in their fight against the Sorcerer King a few months back.

"Your crew works fast," Cortes grunted.

Black-suited figures were moving efficiently through the chaos surrounding the brownstone building housing the *Oro Divino*. They wore badges identifying them as Special Affairs Bureau agents.

"They're not my crew," Jared said curtly. He jerked a thumb at the blown-out windows on the third floor of the restaurant. "We need to talk about what happened up there," the NYPD Lieutenant told Vlad. He stilled, his brow wrinkling. "You look like shit."

"Thanks," Vlad muttered. He started to push himself up.

His legs buckled.

Cortes caught his arm, surprise flashing across his face.

"Hey, take it slow." Concern laced Jared's voice as he moved to the other side of him.

Tarang pressed against Vlad's back, supporting him.

The familiar's confusion and agitation bled through their strained bond. Vlad's heart clenched.

Did those men do something to us?!

Jared glanced at the gathering crowd. "Let's get you somewhere less public."

"I hate to say this, but you look even worse now than you did after you passed out," Cortes told Vlad grimly.

Vlad let them guide him toward a black SUV with government plates. The short walk seemed to take forever, his legs feeling like rubber all the way.

"Lieutenant Dickson!"

A young officer was jogging toward them, his expression keen.

Jared's face hardened. "Not now, Peterson."

"Sir, witnesses are saying they saw the Lucianos and the head of the *Red Dragon* Triad walk into that building—" the officer protested.

"What they saw," Jared cut in sharply, "was a couple of restaurant guests entering the premises before a failed robbery attempt took place. Nothing more."

"But—!" Petersen faltered at Jared's scowl. "Yes, sir."

"Get statements from the crowd," Jared ordered. "Standard procedure."

Peterson walked away, visibly deflated.

"Rookie?" Cortes hazarded.

"Fresh out of the academy." Jared sighed. "He's got a good head on him."

"Give him a month," Cortes said. "He'll soon learn not to ask questions about the weird shit that happens in this city."

Jared's expression grew pinched.

They reached the SUV. Vlad sank gratefully onto the back seat, his body feeling impossibly heavy. Cortes and Tarang climbed in beside him, the familiar's usual grace oddly stilted.

Jared got in the front seat and shut the door, muffling the chaos outside. He turned to face Vlad.

"The agents from the bureau are handling the cleanup, but I need to know what exactly they're cleaning up in there." The Immortal's tone grew careful. "My understanding is the *Black Devils* were brokering a deal between Giovanni Luciano and Wei Chen. What happened?"

Vlad wasn't the least bit surprised the Immortal knew the details of tonight's meeting.

Cortes glanced at him. Vlad nodded, too dizzy to speak.

"We were attacked by a team in tactical gear," Cortes told Jared.

Jared's eyes shrank to slits. "Special ops?"

"I doubt it."

"Was it another organization?" the Immortal grunted.

Cortes frowned. "Hard to tell right now, but that would be at the top of my list."

Vlad had to concur.

"What were you doing in there anyway?" Jared asked the Colombian suspiciously.

Cortes sighed and rubbed the back of his neck. "Yuliy Vissarion asked my ex-boss if I could act as an external observer for the proceedings." He made a face. "It's a good thing he did. An all-out war could have broken out tonight if something had happened to Giovanni or Wei Chen. As it is, Giovanni's son got shot."

Jared cursed. "Is he okay?!"

"He will be."

Jared's troubled gaze switched to Vlad. "You have any idea who could have attacked the building?"

"If you're asking if the *Black Devils* made any new enemies lately, the answer is no," Vlad said tiredly.

He reached for his powers again, desperately hoping his earlier attempts had been a fluke. The void where his magic should have been yawned back at him.

Vlad swallowed as he came to terms with the bitter truth.

"We may not know who they are yet, but I'm pretty sure I was their target."

Jared lowered his brows. "How so?"

"Because I can't use my powers."

Jared blinked. Cortes's eyes flared.

"What do you mean, you can't use your powers?" the Colombian said in a haunted voice. "Did they do something to your core?!" His gaze dropped to Vlad's stomach.

Vlad knew Cortes was thinking back to the time when he had lost his first familiar and his ability to use magic after his aunt attacked him and cracked his core.

"I don't know." Vlad curled his hands into fists. "The only thing I'm certain of right now is I can't access any of my demonic abilities. Neither can Tarang."

The tiger whined softly and pressed closer to him in the stunned silence, their potent bond reduced to a whisper.

"Shit." Cortes slammed a fist against the door, jaw tight and eyes burning. "It must have been that weird magic we felt!"

Jared stared. "What weird magic?"

Cortes told him about the strange power they'd sensed during the attack.

Bile burned the back of Vlad's throat when he recalled the pain that had rendered him senseless.

Jared lowered his brows in the tense hush that ensued. "Vlad's powers are part of his demonic heritage. They're literally woven into his DNA. How could they suppress it?"

A bitter sound left Vlad. "They appear to have done just that."

"But how?" Cortes insisted. "And more importantly, why?"

A knock on the window made them jump.

CHAPTER FIVE

It was Ilya. The bodyguard's face was taut with tension.

Jared lowered the glass. "Should you be walking?" he grunted.

"It's only a flesh wound," Ilya said dismissively. His gaze found Vlad. "We have a situation. Giovanni and Wei Chen are demanding answers."

Vlad's stomach churned.

That doesn't really come as a surprise considering what they witnessed tonight. Hearing rumors about what I can do is one thing. Seeing it in action is a whole other ball game.

"Where are they now?"

"At the precinct, giving their statements. They're sticking to the robbery story Lieutenant Dickson came up with." Ilya hesitated. "There's something else. Someone recorded what happened inside the restaurant. The video's already circulating."

"Fuck," Cortes breathed.

Vlad clenched his teeth. *Dammit! That's the last thing we need right now.*

Having other criminal organizations witness the powers they'd long suspected he had *and* watching him collapse at the end of that battle was going to open a whole other can of worms.

His head throbbed.

Was that those men's endgame all along? To show that the heir to the Black Devils *isn't invincible after all?*

Jared got his phone out and dialed a number. "I'll get it taken down."

Frustration tightened Vlad's chest. He dropped his head against the back rest and closed his eyes again. Under any other circumstance, he would have been the one putting that call out. Except he felt as powerless as a newborn fawn right now.

Ilya spoke again. "Yuliy is on his way."

Vlad's eyes snapped open. "What?!"

"Milo called Gustav," Ilya admitted guiltily. "I'd offer to put a bullet through him, but he's already been shot."

Gustav Luchok was Yuliy's secretary. He'd practically brought Vlad up along with his uncle and Lena Dubravac, their housekeeper.

Vlad swallowed a groan. *Of course Gustav told Yuliy.*

The man was more protective of him than a mother hen.

"Yuliy can't know." Vlad narrowed his eyes at Cortes and Jared. "None of the *Bratva* can know about this. If word gets out that I've lost my powers—"

Ilya froze. "Wait. *You've lost your powers?!*"

They hushed him.

Ilya lowered his voice, his face ashen. "What does that mean?"

"It's exactly as I said." Vlad put a hand on Tarang. His strength was slowly returning and with it the sharp focus that was his trademark. "Neither of us can access our powers. And worse, our bond feels—different. Weaker. Like something is blocking our connection."

Tarang made a pained sound and plopped his head on Vlad's lap.

Vlad's voice hardened. "You know what will happen if word gets out."

He could tell from their expressions that no further explanation was required.

Though many wished to see the demise of crime syndicates, they were essential tools governments and law agencies relied upon to control the more abhorrent transgressors in human society. The *Black Devils* was one such organization, their influence in the New York criminal underworld keeping some of the more ruthless gangs trying to infiltrate the city's lucrative drug and trafficking routes at bay.

Their enemies would see Vlad as their *Bratva's* weakness if they discovered he'd lost his powers. They would start testing boundaries, probing for vulnerabilities. Some might even try to eliminate him altogether, viewing him as an easy target without his rumored demonic abilities.

And that's assuming the Bratva *leadership in Moscow doesn't decide to replace me as Yuliy's heir the moment they find out.*

Vlad's nails dug into his palms at that bitter thought.

There was a time when the last thing he'd wanted was to inherit the heavy mantle worn by his uncle. But he'd seen firsthand the good Yuliy had done while in that role and he was determined to continue his legacy.

"We're going to have to buy some time until we figure out why I lost my powers and how to fix it."

Vlad didn't voice the fear eating at him.

That they might not be able to fix it.

"How about getting Mae to look at your core?" Jared suggested.

Vlad hesitated. It was by far the easiest course of action.

From Cortes's expression, he agreed with Jared.

"Give me a few days to see what we can find out first," Vlad said reluctantly.

Jared frowned. "I'll contain the situation from the law enforcement side. Make sure the official report shows nothing unusual." He paused. "But the crime families are another matter. You can't undo what they saw."

"There *is* one way to deal with that situation," Cortes said slowly.

Vlad's pulse quickened. *Anya.*

The witch's Illusion Sorcery could easily undo Giovanni's and Wei Chen's memories.

Jared grimaced. "How about we don't mess with the heads of people who can bring an ugly war to the streets of this city?"

"Leave Giovanni and Wei Chen to me," Vlad said grimly. "I'll find a way to deal with them."

He had no idea how he was going to handle them, but he'd figure something out. He had to.

The sound of helicopter rotors filled the air.

They looked outside.

A sleek black helicopter was descending toward a nearby rooftop, the Vissarion family crest visible on its side.

"Yuliy's here," Ilya said unnecessarily.

Vlad grimaced.

He must think I'm at death's door if he took the helicopter.

He steeled himself before climbing out of the vehicle with Tarang and the others. His legs were steadier this time, though his body still felt wrong.

Tarang brushed against him, their damaged connection humming with shared anxiety.

Vlad clenched his jaw.

He had to convince his uncle nothing was wrong with them.

Cortes studied him, troubled. "You sure you can do this? You still look like death warmed over."

"I don't really have a choice," Vlad muttered.

They crossed the street toward the building where the helicopter was shutting off its engine. The diamond studs in Vlad's ears caught his eye as they reflected off a window they passed. The weapons had remained stubbornly inert despite his silent commands.

This left him feeling even more vulnerable.

The helicopter had landed on top of a parking structure. Its rotors were slowing as Vlad and Ilya climbed the access stairs and emerged onto the rooftop, Cortes and Jared following at a discreet distance.

Yuliy Vissarion stepped out of the aircraft, his clothes whipping in the downdraft. Though in his sixties, Vlad's uncle still exuded a formidable presence. His silver hair caught the emergency lights as his sharp gaze found them.

Gustav climbed out after him. The secretary's usually unflappable demeanor evaporated at the sight of Vlad. He hurried over.

"Are you alright?"

"I'm fine." Vlad managed a reassuring smile. "Just a few bruises."

It wasn't exactly a lie. His body ached all over.

Yuliy's scrutiny felt like a physical weight as he approached. He embraced Vlad, his arms squeezing him tightly.

Vlad knew the older man was anxious, even if he didn't show it.

Yuliy let go and stepped back. "What happened?"

"We think it might have been a professional hit squad," Vlad lied proficiently. "At least fifteen men. They came through the windows during the negotiations." He glanced at Cortes over his shoulder.

Cortes nodded, poker-faced.

Yuliy dipped his head at the Colombian. "I hear you helped. You have my gratitude."

Cortes shrugged. "You can add it to my tab."

Yuliy's gaze switched to Vlad. "The Lucianos and Wei Chen?"

"They're safe. Ilya got everyone out."

Some of the tension left Yuliy's shoulders. "Any casualties?"

"A few of our men took hits, including Ilya and Milo," Vlad replied. "Marco Luciano caught a bullet, but he'll live."

Yuliy and Gustav stared at Ilya.

"You took a bullet?" Concern laced Yuliy's voice.

He and Ilya went back a long way.

"Missed my ass by a few inches," Ilya grunted.

Yuliy ran a hand through his hair. "The whole point of tonight was to prove we could maintain peace between the families." His mouth flattened to a thin line. "Looks like we failed spectacularly."

Vlad's jaw tightened. "I'm sorry."

Yuliy lowered his brows. "I'm not blaming you. It's clear this was an orchestrated attack. We need to find out who's behind it and what their aim is before the fallout buries us."

Vlad could feel Cortes's and Jared's gazes burning a hole in the back of his head.

"I'm afraid I have more bad news."

Yuliy sighed. "Let me guess. The Lucianos and Wei Chen saw something they shouldn't have?"

Vlad nodded. "Tarang manifested his presence during the fight. And Cortes and I used our powers."

Yuliy rubbed his chin slowly. "We can handle the families," he said after a moment. "It's not ideal, but it won't be the first time we've had to explain things to outsiders."

"There's something else." Vlad's nails dug into his palms. "Someone recorded the incident and posted the video online."

Yuliy froze. He cursed viciously in Russian in the next instant.

Gustav's eyes had darkened, the deadly focus that

made him Yuliy's right-hand man returning to his face. "How much did they capture?"

"All of it," Jared grunted. "The video is already down. But a lot of people saw it."

Gustav took his cell out and started calling people, his expression somber.

Yuliy observed Vlad critically. "Go home and get some rest. I'll send some men to watch over your place."

Vlad opened his mouth to protest.

"That wasn't a suggestion." His uncle's eyes softened slightly. "Whatever else happened tonight, you kept your word. The families are alive. Let me deal with the politics."

It was a dismissal, albeit a gentle one.

Vlad nodded reluctantly. "Yes, *dyadya*."

He turned to leave.

"I'll assign you a new bodyguard," Yuliy said. "Ilya and Milo will be out of action for a while."

Ilya protested.

Yuliy cut his eyes to him. "You either take the time you need to heal or I'll put another bullet through your leg."

"Yes, boss," Ilya murmured miserably.

"I don't need a babysitter," Vlad said irritably. "I have Tarang."

Tarang yowled, similarly incensed.

"Really?" Cortes muttered behind him. "You two want to have that argument right now?"

Yuliy's eyes shrank to slits. "You're having a bodyguard and that's that."

Vlad ground his teeth. *Great. Just great.*

CHAPTER SIX

THE NOISE AND HEAT OF THE BAR WASHED PLEASANTLY OVER Vlad as he lounged in a red leather armchair.

Though it was a welcome respite from the chaos of the past couple of days, the whiskey in his glass did nothing to ease the hollowness inside him. He took a brooding sip of his drink and watched the patrons milling about.

The *Velvet Room* was a high-end bar a few blocks from his Chelsea penthouse. The place had a retro vibe, all dark wood and leather, and an impressive collection of rare spirits displayed behind a copper-topped bar.

It was one of his regular haunts for those nights when he didn't want to be alone in his apartment.

Tarang paced restlessly beside his chair. Though invisible to the crowd in the bar, his familiar's anxiety was all too apparent to Vlad, his emotion bleeding through their dull bond.

Forty-eight hours after the incident at the *Oro Divino*, they still couldn't access their powers.

"You're going to wear a hole in that rug," Cortes told the tiger.

Tarang made an annoyed sound.

The Colombian was nursing his own drink opposite Vlad, his relaxed pose that of a man without a care in the world. Only someone who knew him well would notice the slight tension in his shoulders.

"How'd the meeting with Giovanni and Wei Chen go?"

Vlad grimaced. "About as well as you'd expect."

The crime lords had been surprisingly amenable to his explanations concerning what had gone down that night. Giovanni had even waved away his son's injuries as an unfortunate consequence of being in their line of business. As for Wei Chen, the Triad leader had been unusually calm as she'd listened to the carefully edited story he'd given them about the powers he, Cortes, and their familiars had demonstrated.

Whether their demeanor was down to his ability to lie through his bare teeth or their own self-preservation instincts in the face of what they'd witnessed remained to be seen.

That might change the moment they find out I've lost my powers.

Cortes's grunt brought him back to the present. "Meaning?"

"Meaning they've agreed to keep quiet about what they saw." Vlad paused. "For now."

Cortes's expression grew shrewd. "And the price for their silence?"

Vlad sighed. "They want a bigger cut of the dock revenues."

Cortes snorted. "Of course they do."

"Yuliy will deal with it." Vlad's grip tightened on his glass. "It's better than the alternative."

Cortes narrowed his eyes. "The alternative being the crime families spreading word that the *Black Devils*' heir is now expendable?"

"Bingo. Though after that video leaked, the damage is already done."

Tarang made a worried sound and bumped his leg.

Vlad instinctively tried to comfort him with a subtle wave of demonic magic. His gut clenched when his attempt returned nothing, his power as inaccessible as it had remained for the past two days.

Popo stirred on Cortes's shoulder.

"You two are looking mighty gloomy tonight," the familiar said merrily, his bright gaze swinging from Vlad to Tarang. "Cheer up, buttercups."

"Not now, Bird Brain," Cortes warned.

The parrot subsided with a put-upon sigh. "I'm only trying to lighten the atmosphere, my Enrique."

"Has Mrs. Son-Ha gotten back to you?" Vlad asked Cortes.

"Not yet. I've had a couple of men camped outside her place for the last couple of days. There's been no sign of her." The Colombian grimaced. "You know how she is. She'll call when she's good and ready."

Vlad wrinkled his brow and rubbed the back of his neck tiredly.

They'd decided the South Korean Shaman was their best chance at figuring out what kind of magic had been used on him. But getting hold of the old woman was like trying to catch smoke with your bare hands.

There's always Bryony Cross. But I'm loath to ask her.

Though she was a good friend of his, the High Priestess of the New York coven was bound to tell Mae what had happened.

Movement at the bar a few feet away caught Vlad's eye.

He looked up and froze, his breath catching.

The woman was six feet tall, with an athletic build that suggested serious hours spent training. Her eyes were a deep sapphire blue and her blonde hair was pulled back in a French braid that emphasized her striking cheekbones and full lips. But it was the way she held herself that drew his attention. Like a predator at rest.

She wore fitted black pants and a cream sweater that did nothing to hide her curves. A leather jacket was draped over the barstool beside her.

Cortes followed his gaze. "That's the most interest you've shown in anything for four whole months." The Colombian's voice held a hint of amusement.

Vlad barely heard him. He was too busy watching the woman deal with the drunk who'd decided to try his luck.

"Come on, gorgeous." The guy who'd approached the blonde was doing his best to crowd her space, his friends loitering a short distance away. "Let me buy you a drink."

She didn't even look at him. "No, thank you."

The drunk frowned slightly at her flat tone.

"Don't be like that. I'm a nice guy," he hiccuped.

"Nice guys generally take no for an answer the first time."

Her voice was low and smooth, touched with an accent Vlad couldn't quite place.

French, maybe?

The drunk's face hardened. He grabbed her arm. "Listen here, you stuck-up bi—"

What happened next was too fast for the human eye to follow.

One moment the guy was reaching for her, the next he was face down on the bar with his arm twisted behind his back. His friends gasped.

"Here's the thing about being nice," the blonde said, maintaining her deadpan tone and expression. "It's a choice. Just like being a moron with a death wish is also a choice." She applied slightly more pressure. The drunk whimpered. "Which choice are you going to make?"

"The nice one!" the drunk squeaked. "Definitely the nice one!"

"Glad we had this chat." She released him. "Now, please leave."

The drunk scuttled away, his friends quickly following.

"Damn," Cortes muttered. "She's good."

Vlad had to agree. The blonde's movements had been fluid and precise.

Almost too precise for a civilian.

Tarang's attention was riveted by the woman. Vlad caught an echo of his familiar's curiosity.

She returned to her drink as if nothing had happened. The bartender approached cautiously.

"Everything okay, miss?"

"Peachy." She paused. "Though you might want to

check your door policy. That guy's cologne alone should be grounds for refusal."

The bartender smiled. "Can I get you another drink? On the house."

She arched a delicate eyebrow. "I never say no to free whiskey."

Vlad couldn't drag his eyes away. Something about her drew him like a moth to a flame. He couldn't remember the last time he'd felt this much genuine interest in someone.

Not since Mae—

He shut that thought down hard.

"Go talk to her," Cortes said.

"I don't know if you noticed, but I'm not exactly myself right now," Vlad muttered.

It wasn't just his missing powers. His confidence had taken a serious hit following the incident at the *Oro Divino*.

Cortes rolled his eyes. "Your charm isn't all demon magic. Some of it is actually you."

"My Enrique speaks the truth," Popo chimed in. "Besides, your pheromone levels indicate you're in optimal condition for mat—*mmph!*"

Cortes had muzzled the parrot.

Vlad grimaced. "Your familiar needs therapy."

"Tell me something I don't know." Cortes frowned at the bird before jerking his head toward the bar. "Seriously though, go. The worst she can do is say no."

Or snap my arm like a twig. But Vlad was already rising to his feet.

Tarang moved to follow. Vlad hesitated.

His familiar usually made himself scarce during his hookups. But something in Tarang's steadfast gaze told him the tiger wasn't going anywhere tonight.

He crossed the floor to the bar, aware of Cortes and Popo watching with poorly concealed interest. Though the woman didn't look up as he approached, the way she fractionally adjusted her posture suggested she knew exactly where he was.

"That was impressive." Vlad settled onto the stool beside her.

Tarang plopped down on his haunches and stared unblinkingly at the blonde.

She glanced at Vlad. "The part where I said no or the part where I had to demonstrate why no means no?"

"The part where you did it without spilling your drink."

That earned him a faintly interested look. "A woman has her priorities."

The bartender appeared with her whiskey. Vlad ordered the same.

The man dipped his head cautiously at him before vanishing.

Most people who worked around here had an inkling who he was.

Though the blonde clocked the exchange, she didn't comment on it.

"Good choice." She studied the amber liquid in her glass. "Though I prefer the twenty-one-year-old myself."

"So do I." He held out his hand. "Vlad."

She eyed it for a moment before taking it. Her grip was

firm, her palm callused in places that confirmed his suspicions about her.

"Delphine."

Looks like I was right about that accent.

They sipped their drinks for a quiet moment.

"What brings you to New York?" Vlad said lightly, watching her reflection in the mirror opposite the bar over the rim of his glass.

She raised an eyebrow. "Who says I'm visiting?"

He smiled at the repartee. "I don't live far from this place. I would have noticed you a long time ago if you were a regular."

Delphine observed him with a quiet intensity that would have made any other man fidget.

"Work," she said finally. "Though tonight I'm just killing time until I get my assignment."

Vlad glanced at her glass. "Must be an important assignment if you're drinking the good stuff."

"More like one I could have done without." Her gaze remained steady, like she was gauging him against some kind of mental checklist. "What about you? You don't strike me as someone who needs to drink alone."

"Who says I'm drinking alone?"

Her gaze moved briefly to where Cortes sat. "Your friend's been checking his phone for the past five minutes. I'm guessing he's about to make his excuses and leave."

On cue, Cortes appeared at Vlad's shoulder.

"Sorry to interrupt." The Colombian didn't even try to hide his amusement as he dipped his head courteously at Delphine. "I'm heading out. Anya called."

Vlad strongly suspected that was a lie.

Popo bobbed on Cortes's shoulder. "Remember what I said about optimal mating conditions—*ow!*"

The parrot rubbed his beak where Cortes had flicked it.

Delphine's gaze narrowed ever so slightly. Though it was clear she couldn't see or hear the bird, her instincts obviously told her something was amiss.

Cortes leaned in to whisper in Vlad's ear. "Don't do anything I wouldn't do."

"That's a very short list," he grunted.

Cortes chuckled and clapped his back before heading for the exit. "I'll text you tomorrow." He waved over his shoulder.

Delphine's gaze returned to Vlad. "Now you really are drinking alone."

"Not anymore," Vlad drawled. He raised his glass.

The blonde smiled faintly and clinked hers against his. "Smooth."

Vlad shrugged. "I try."

He couldn't help stare as she took another sip of her drink. The way she moved was riveting, every gesture deliberate and on point. Like she was constantly aware of her body and the space around her.

Even the way she swallowed fascinated him.

Tarang prowled closer, his curiosity a faint, warm pulse through their bond. To Vlad's surprise, the tiger settled near Delphine's feet, head cocked as he studied her.

"Military?" Vlad hazarded.

Delphine crunched on an ice cube. "What makes you say that?"

"The way you handled that drunk. That wasn't some self-defense class move."

She shrugged. "Maybe I just work out a lot." Her stare turned piercing. "What about you? You move like someone who knows how to handle himself."

CHAPTER SEVEN

Vlad discerned the hidden question in her words.

"I box." It wasn't exactly a lie. "It keeps me grounded."

Delphine cocked her head. "Somehow I doubt that." She considered him for a moment. "So, what's your story? Besides drinking good whiskey and making conversation with strange women in bars?"

Vlad's mouth curved. "Would you believe I'm independently wealthy and spend my days collecting rare books?"

"No," she replied stoically.

"How about running an underground fight club?"

"Getting warmer." She took another sip of her drink. "I'm guessing the reality is more complicated."

Vlad's smile turned wry. "Isn't it always?"

Something sparked between them then, hot and electric.

Vlad's pulse spiked. He hadn't felt anything like it since—

Yeah, best not go there.

Delphine focused fully on him, like she could sense the attraction sizzling between them and was debating what to do about it.

"You know what I think?"

"What's that?" Vlad said almost breathlessly.

"I think you're trouble."

Heat pooled in Vlad's veins at the banked heat in her gaze.

"Good trouble or bad trouble?" he said, his tone dropping an octave.

She didn't miss his attempt to seduce her. "Is there a difference?"

"Usually. Sometimes the line gets blurry."

Delphine studied him over the rim of her glass, something knowing in her expression. "I get the feeling you're speaking from experience."

"Maybe." Vlad arched an eyebrow, emboldened by the smoldering fire in her eyes. "Want to find out?"

A hint of amusement pulled at the corners of Delphine's mouth. "Are you propositioning me?"

"That depends."

"On what?"

"Whether you're saying yes."

A bark of laughter left her then, the sound surprising her as much as it did him. She shook her head, her cheeks dimpling. "You really are trouble."

"You haven't answered my question."

Delphine drummed her fingers on the bar. She came to a decision, set her glass down, and turned to face him fully. Her knee brushed his thigh, the contact sending sparks dancing along his nerve endings.

"Here's the thing," she said slightly coolly. "I make it a rule not to go home with strangers."

"We're not strangers." Vlad gave her his most charming smile. "We've been drinking together for at least twenty minutes."

Delphine rolled her eyes a little. "Ah, yes. Practically bosom buddies."

Vlad cocked his head toward where Cortes had been sitting. "I even introduced you to my friend."

"Your friend with the weird habit of flicking at imaginary things?"

Vlad nearly choked on his whiskey.

Damn. She's good.

"Speaking of imaginary things." Delphine glanced down, her gaze landing exactly where Tarang sat.

The tiger went still.

Vlad's heartbeat quickened. There was no way she could actually see his familiar. But something in her expression made him wonder.

"Yes?" he said carefully.

Delphine met his eyes again. "Your place or mine? I'm staying at a hotel close by."

The sudden shift threw him. He stared.

"What happened to not going home with strangers?"

"What can I say?" She rose, her movements graceful. "I'm feeling rebellious."

Vlad put his glass down and stood up.

Delphine came up to his height thanks to her boots. It was oddly thrilling.

"My place is probably closer," he said.

She bobbed her head. "Let's go."

He helped her into her leather jacket and used the excuse to brush his fingers against her neck. Her skin was warm, her pulse steady beneath his touch.

Usually, his incubus powers would tell him exactly what effect he was having on a potential lover. But even without that advantage, he could sense Delphine's sexual interest. It was there in the way she leaned ever so slightly into his touch and the gleam in her eyes when she looked at him.

They settled their tab and headed for the door. The night air was crisp, hinting at the spring to come.

"This way." Vlad indicated the direction of his apartment.

Delphine fell into step beside him, her stride matching his easily. Tarang padded silently after them, the tiger still watching the blonde with unusual intensity.

It didn't take them long to reach his apartment building.

"Let me guess." She glanced at him as they approached the converted industrial warehouse with its restored redbrick facade. "Penthouse?"

Vlad raised an eyebrow. "What makes you think that?"

"You wear expensive suits, drink rare whiskey, and smell of old money." Delphine shrugged. "Plus, this is Chelsea. Real estate doesn't come cheap around here."

I better not tell her I own the entire building.

"Maybe I'm just really good at what I do," Vlad said lightly.

"Oh, I'm certain you are." Her sultry tone made his

blood heat. "Though I am curious what, exactly, it is you do."

Vlad clocked the *Black Devils'* SUVs guarding the premises as they came in sight of the entrance. He caught Delphine's hand and pulled her closer, hoping to distract her.

"Tonight, I'm planning to make you forget all about that assignment you came to New York for."

"Confident, aren't you?"

Vlad arched an eyebrow. "I'm full of surprises."

Fire sparked in Delphine's eyes.

The doorman nodded respectfully when they entered the marble lobby.

"Definitely the penthouse," she murmured.

Vlad shot her an amused look as they stepped into a private elevator, Tarang keeping close to him. "You sound pretty sure about that."

"I notice things." She crossed her arms and leaned against the wall, watching him through half-lidded eyes. "Like how that doorman definitely had a gun under his jacket. And how there are more security cameras than this place should need. Oh, and let's not forget the guard dogs parked outside."

Vlad stiffened. Before he could analyze whether her words were a threat, Delphine closed the distance between them. She grabbed the lapels of his suit, tugged him close, and pressed her mouth to his.

Her kiss stole his breath. She tasted like expensive whiskey, her body fitting against his like she belonged there.

Vlad buried his hands in her hair and deepened the

kiss, loving the feel of her against him. Delphine made a sound low in her throat that shot straight to his groin.

The elevator dinged.

They reluctantly ended the kiss. Delphine's lips were slightly swollen, desire turning her eyes the color of a stormy sea.

"Coming?" she said as she stepped out of the elevator.

He grinned, the double entendre not lost on him as he followed her across the landing to his apartment.

Tarang slipped quietly through the front door when Vlad opened it. The tiger's subdued behavior roused his curiosity once more.

Delphine hooked her fingers into his belt loops.

He chuckled as she pulled him into the penthouse foyer, only for his breath to catch when his back hit the wall.

Delphine's mouth found his again, hungry and demanding.

Her strength surprised him.

It was as if a switch had flipped inside her and she was showing him her true self for the first time that night.

"Bedroom?" she breathed against his lips.

"Upstairs." Vlad caught her hips and used the leverage to reverse their positions, making her gasp softly. "Unless you'd prefer the couch?"

Color stained her cheekbones when she felt the evidence of his desire.

"Bed." She leaned in and tugged his lower lip sultrily with her teeth before releasing him. "I plan to take my time with you."

Heat smoldered in Vlad's veins. He was usually the one

who took control during encounters like this. But something about Delphine made him want to cede that control.

They left a trail of clothes in their wake as they made their way up the stairs, their hands urgent and their mouths meeting in hungry kisses. Delphine's sweater hit his antique sideboard. His jacket and tie joined it. Her boots ended up somewhere near his bedroom.

Vlad closed the door on an annoyed Tarang's face and took a moment to appreciate the black lace underneath Delphine's clothes before she dragged him across the floor and pushed him onto his bed. He went willingly, drinking in the sight of her crawling up his body.

"Nice digs." Her gaze swept the masculine surroundings before finding his, the heat in her eyes incandescent. "Still feeling confident?"

He laughed. The sound turned into a groan when she rolled her hips.

"Getting more confident by the second!" he gasped.

The slow smile Delphine gave him was pure sin. "Good."

Vlad forgot about everything as the night wore on and he lost himself to the woman in his arms.

His missing powers. The mess with the crime families. Mae.

It wasn't until they finally fell asleep in a tangle of limbs, sweat cooling off their sated bodies, that he realized he felt like himself again for the first time in months.

It seemed like barely minutes had passed before sunlight was warming his face, dragging him from a deep slumber. His body ached pleasantly, memories of the night's activities bringing a smile to his lips even before he opened his eyes.

He reached across the bed.

The sheets beside him were cool.

Vlad's eyes snapped open. He sat up and scanned the room.

There was no sign of Delphine.

If not for the rumpled sheets and the lingering scent of her perfume on his pillow, he might have thought he'd dreamed the whole thing.

Vlad slumped and scrubbed a hand over his face, torn between disappointment and grudging admiration. Delphine had managed to slip out without him noticing, something he suspected might have happened even if he'd been in full possession of his demonic powers.

Guess she only wanted a one-night stand.

He dropped back down on the pillow and stared at the ceiling.

On a scale of one to ten, last night had been a solid one hundred. A dry smile stretched his lips. He'd almost struggled to keep up with Delphine's stamina without his incubus powers.

She really was something.

The chances that they would meet again was pretty much nil. Vlad had no doubt Delphine would not visit the *Velvet Room* while she remained in New York for business.

He climbed out of bed and hit the shower, determined to put the encounter behind him.

It had been a spectacular night and it would make for a great memory.

It wasn't until he was adjusting his silk tie moments

later that he realized something that stunned him. Vlad's hand stilled.

The hollow feeling he'd carried inside him after losing Mae to Nikolai had all but faded.

He stared at his reflection in the floor-length mirror in his dressing room.

Have I moved on from her?

He knew he would always hold a deep affection for Mae. But the wound she had inadvertently carved into his heart felt like it was finally healing.

Vlad wondered whether the woman he'd just spent the night with had anything to do with it.

I guess I'll never find out, since I'm not going to see her again.

He exited the dressing room, his steps light. Tarang was sprawled in a patch of sunlight on the landing when he opened the bedroom door.

"You could have warned me she was leaving," Vlad told the tiger drily.

Tarang huffed guiltily.

"Come on." Vlad headed for the stairs. "Let's get you some breakfast."

Tarang licked his chops and rose to follow him.

Vlad's phone buzzed as he was pouring himself a coffee.

It was Gustav, reminding him that he had to be at Yuliy's mansion at ten a.m. to meet his new bodyguard.

CHAPTER EIGHT

Delphine turned her black Range Rover onto a private road in Mill Basin, her mind still full of the man whose bed she'd left that morning.

Vlad's kisses. His hands in her hair and on her body. The way he'd moved above and beneath her, his face flushed with pleasure and his fingers holding her hips firmly in place as they'd made love.

He'd tasted like sin and promises she should never have been tempted by.

Delphine frowned.

One-night stands were not really her thing.

She'd even debated whether to leave Vlad her phone number that morning, a thought that would normally never have crossed her mind in a million years. One look at his arresting face, his broad back, and the alluring lines of his ass under the black silk sheets was all it had taken for desire to sing through her blood once more.

Sex with Vlad was something she could easily get addicted to.

She'd grabbed her clothes and left before she did something she would come to regret. Their encounter would remain just that. A one-night stand.

Her belly clenched.

Let's face it, it was the best night of my life.

Her existence as a super soldier rarely afforded the luxury of a relationship. Nothing had made this clearer than Gideon Morgan's phone call yesterday morning, just as she was finishing her workout in her DC apartment.

"I need you in New York," the super soldier who led the mercenary corps she belonged to had said without preamble.

"I thought that was Serena's territory now." Delphine had continued her cool-down stretches, phone on speaker.

Serena Blake was a member of their brethren and a close friend. Though a mere handful of years separated them, Serena still remembered when she and Nate Conway, their brother-in-arms, were rescued by the Immortals in Greenland when they were still children. Delphine had still been an infant at the time and had no memories of the gruesome experiments a group of Immortals backed by a rogue group of the US government had performed on them from their inception.

"That was a temporary arrangement," Gideon had said. "I need you to protect someone and assist with an investigation."

Delphine had paused mid-stretch, her brow wrinkling. "That's not usually my thing."

"It is now."

Something in his tone had made her pay attention. Gideon didn't get rattled easily.

"What's the catch?"

"The client will brief you," Gideon had said, neatly sidestepping the question. He'd given her an address. "Be there tomorrow at ten. And Del?"

"Yeah?"

"Watch yourself on this one."

It wasn't like Gideon to be so cryptic. Which meant this assignment was like few she'd ever handled before.

Delphine had memorized the address. Particulars about the actual mission remained conspicuously absent, however. No briefing package or dossier followed, even after she reached New York.

I guess he was right about the client briefing me directly.

Searching for the address in the super soldier database she had access to had brought up nothing. Even the Immortals' sophisticated satellite network had drawn a blank, the area she was interested in examining made to look like empty marshland.

The tinted windows of the vehicle offered her a measure of privacy as she approached the meeting place. She studied her surroundings curiously.

The road ended at a pair of metal gates set in a steel-reinforced concrete wall encircling an estate. Trees lined both sides of the drive, their branches forming a natural barrier between the property and the rest of Brooklyn.

A metal post rose from the ground as she pulled to a stop in front of the entrance. It flipped open to reveal a small black cube. A red-light grid scanned her face.

"Please identify yourself."

"Delphine Dubois." Her tone matched the AI's cool efficiency. "I have a ten a.m. appointment."

The computer processed this for a couple of seconds before the post and the black cube retracted into the ground. The gates rolled open on well-oiled hinges.

She followed a cream-colored concrete driveway as it wound through the grounds, her eye noting the security measures she could see. Dozens of cameras tracked her progress. Guards patrolled the grounds. Someone had even positioned the ornamental trees to eliminate blind spots.

Delphine pursed her lips.

Whoever lives here isn't just wealthy. They're either paranoid as hell or have good reason for this level of security.

She already had an inkling about her client's day job. Time would tell if her instincts proved to be correct.

They usually were.

The trees finally parted, revealing what they'd been hiding. Delphine's hands tightened fractionally on the steering wheel.

The mansion rising ahead of her wasn't just a home. It was a statement of power. The buildings formed several wings that crowned a shallow elevation, their glass and white concrete facades gleaming in the morning sun. Extensive terraced gardens surrounded the property, leading down to a private marina and a helicopter landing pad.

It was obvious why someone had gone to considerable trouble to keep this place off the radar.

A garage complex came into view. It housed an

impressive collection of vehicles, including a fleet of black SUVs similar to hers.

Delphine was now pretty certain she was dealing with a mobster. What kind of job required her specific skill set in a place like this, she still wasn't sure. After all, crime lords could afford bodyguards like nobody's business. Someone seeking a super soldier for the role had to either have some seriously nasty enemies or the kind of problem normal people couldn't handle.

Vlad's face danced before her eyes as she parked the Range Rover next to a midnight-blue Bentley convertible.

There had been a moment last night when she'd wondered if he belonged to the criminal underworld. He was too suave. Too smooth. Too...*good looking* to hold down any other kind of job.

Delphine berated herself at that random thought.

Focus.

She stepped out of the Range Rover, conscious of at least a dozen pairs of eyes watching her movements. The front steps of the mansion were white marble. Delphine climbed them, noting the discreet security panels beside the bronze doors.

They opened before she could knock. A man in his fifties stood in the entrance, his charcoal suit hiding the gun under his left armpit and the knife strapped to his right ankle.

"Miss Dubois." The stranger's face gave nothing away. "Welcome to the Vissarion residence. I'm Gustav Luchok, Mr. Vissarion's secretary." He dipped his head and beckoned her inside with a dignified movement.

Delphine's scalp prickled as she crossed the threshold.

The name Vissarion had featured prominently in a briefing Gideon had recently given them on the latest developments in New York's criminal underworld. Serena had also referenced the name when they'd spoken a few months ago.

They are the leading Bratva *on the East Coast.*

She masked her wariness and concentrated on her surroundings.

The entrance hall was cavernous, all clean lines and pale stone. A grand staircase dominated the space, bifurcating at a main landing before rising to the upper floors.

A woman appeared silently behind Gustav. Though well past retirement age, she moved with the grace of someone much younger. Her gray hair was pinned in an austere bun and her dark dress whispered against the marble floor.

"This is Lena Dubravac," Gustav said. "She runs the household."

Delphine nodded politely. Lena dipped her chin gracefully.

The way the pair carried themselves made it clear they were more than just staff.

"This way, please." Gustav indicated the interior of the house.

Delphine followed him through the modern interior as they headed into the east wing, her gaze categorizing escape routes and defensive positions out of habit. The decor was ultramodern and minimalistic, everything expensive but chosen with care. Like the security measures outside, nothing was what it initially appeared to be.

Gustav stopped before a door and knocked.

"Come in," a voice called out.

The secretary opened the door and led the way inside.

The study Delphine entered was decorated along the same clinical lines as the rest of the mansion. The only splash of color was a vibrant red Diaspro marble wall framing the fireplace, its surface rich with black and cream veins.

Her gaze found the man behind the desk first. Silver-haired, sharp-eyed. Scars on the back of his hands.

Power radiated from Yuliy Vissarion like heat from a furnace.

A figure was slowly rising from one of the Chesterfield sofas next to the open fire.

Her step didn't falter. Her expression didn't change.

But something inside her went very still.

Vlad's eyes met hers. Unlike her, he didn't quite manage to hide his shock.

CHAPTER NINE

For the first time in his life, Vlad's perfect composure nearly cracked.

His mind froze at the sight of Delphine standing in his uncle's study, the blonde looking as coolly professional in her fitted black suit as she had been passionately wild in his bed mere hours ago.

Instinct had him reaching for his incubus powers to steady himself. The maddening void where his magic should be mocked him instead. His pulse thundered in his ears, his palms growing damp in a way they never had before he'd lost his abilities.

Tarang made a worried sound beside him.

Memories of last night flashed through Vlad's mind. Little things he'd dismissed at the time now took on new significance. How Delphine had noticed details about his building's security. The way her gaze had lingered on Tarang's invisible presence. Her movements when she'd dealt with the drunk at the bar.

"Vlad." Yuliy's voice cut through his spiraling thoughts. "This is Delphine Dubois. She'll be your new protection detail while Ilya and Milo are out of action. She's also be assisting us with our investigation. Miss Dubois, this is my nephew, Vlad."

The protest tearing up Vlad's throat died on his lips. He knew his uncle had been insistent about the whole bodyguard situation, but this was the last thing he'd expected.

"Mr. Vissarion." Delphine nodded curtly at him, her tone pure professional courtesy that betrayed nothing of their recent encounter. Her control only served to emphasize how badly he was floundering. She addressed him and Yuliy. "I appreciate you considering me for this position."

Vlad almost blurted that he'd had nothing to do with it. He took a shallow breath and gained rigid control over his emotions.

He discovered he didn't want Delphine to gain the upper hand.

Tarang was studying the blonde unblinkingly, as fascinated with her as he had been last night.

"Please, sit." Yuliy indicated the leather armchairs facing him. "We have much to discuss."

Vlad forced his feet to move, acutely conscious of Delphine's presence as he settled into the chair beside her. Her perfume, the same scent that still clung to his sheets, teased his senses. He clenched his jaw.

She crossed her legs, the movement drawing his eye before he caught himself. He looked up and found her watching him with that same intensity she'd shown at the bar last night, except now there was nothing but cool detachment behind it.

Yuliy's sharp gaze moved between them, like he could sense the underlying tension crackling between them. Gustav stared.

There was a soft knock at the door. It opened to reveal Lena and a tea cart packed with freshly-baked muffins and croissants.

"Miss Dubois comes highly recommended," Yuliy told Vlad as the housekeeper began serving them a light breakfast. "She's perfect for this job."

"With all due respect, Mr. Vissarion," Delphine said as she accepted a cup of tea from Lena, "I received very little information about this assignment. Even my employer was unusually vague about the details."

Though her tone remained measured and businesslike, Vlad detected a trace of tension in her shoulders.

Not so calm after all.

The knowledge that he could read her sent a measure of relief through Vlad that made him freeze with his next heartbeat.

Wait. What am I thinking right now? I shouldn't be giving a damn whether she's calm or not!

His fingers whitened on his cup. There wasn't a single good reason for him to be annoyed with the woman sitting beside him. He was positive she'd had no idea who he was when he'd approached her at the bar.

Yet he couldn't ignore the feeling of betrayal gnawing at his insides.

Delphine cut her eyes to him for a fraction of a second. Last night, he'd attributed her observational skills to her probable military background. Now he wondered what else she could see behind the mask he carefully projected to the world.

"I'm afraid that's entirely my fault," Yuliy told Delphine apologetically. "I made Mr. Morgan promise not to give you any details concerning the...sensitive nature of this mission."

The name Yuliy had spoken made Vlad straighten in his chair.

"Morgan? As in Gideon Morgan?!" His gaze swung from Yuliy to Delphine, his pulse quickening.

He knew of the mercenary. Gideon Morgan headed a team of elite super soldiers who'd carried out more dangerous missions in the last decade than any other special ops team in the world. He was the guy who'd sent Serena Blake to New York a few months ago, after the Sorcerer King had captured Nikolai.

"Do you know Serena?" Vlad asked Delphine stiffly.

She nodded curtly. "We are close friends."

Vlad's stomach knotted as he recalled her strength from last night.

"Does that mean you're a super soldier?"

"I am." Delphine arched an eyebrow. "Is that going to be a problem?"

"No, it isn't." Yuliy was frowning at Vlad.

Even Gustav and Lena were giving him puzzled looks.

Vlad lowered his brows at his uncle. "When you said you were going to get me a new bodyguard, I didn't know it would be a super soldier."

"Considering the circumstances, Miss Dubois is the best person for the job," Yuliy retorted in a hard voice. "In fact, her expertise makes her uniquely qualified for this position."

A vein throbbed in Vlad's temple.

"She doesn't know the nature of what she might have to deal with."

Yuliy gave him an obtuse look that indicated he knew exactly what Vlad was talking about and didn't give a damn.

A shadow passed over Delphine's face, there and gone so quickly Vlad almost missed it.

She's annoyed.

"Maybe if you elaborated on the details, it would help me reassure you of my capabilities," she told Vlad steadily.

The last thread of Vlad's patience snapped at the silent challenge in her eyes.

"Tarang," he growled. "Show yourself."

Delphine went deathly still when the tiger suddenly made himself visible beside her chair.

Yuliy sighed.

Gustav pinched the bridge of his nose and muttered something under his breath.

"You could at least have given her a warning," Lena snapped at Vlad.

Tarang plopped his head on his giant paws and watched Delphine unblinkingly, his tail sweeping the floor in a lazy rhythm that said he was willing to be buddies if she was.

"That's a big tiger," Delphine stated with a sangfroid that Vlad couldn't help but admire despite the irritation prickling his skin.

To everyone's surprise, she leaned over and placed her

hand calmly in front of the familiar so he could get used to her scent.

Tarang sniffed her skin and carefully licked her pinky.

Lena hid a small smile. Approval glittered in Yuliy's and Gustav's eyes.

Anyone Tarang liked was a keeper in their books.

Delphine watched the familiar for a moment before meeting Vlad's gaze. "Are you a sorcerer?"

The question startled him. He fisted his hands.

He knew he would have hidden his reaction better had he been in possession of his incubus powers.

"You know about witches and sorcerers?"

Delphine shrugged. "A bit. Serena is acquainted with a bunch of them. She married the son of a demon after all and lives with a bunch of divine beasts in Chicago, a fact I believe you are aware of after meeting her a few months ago."

Wariness crept onto Yuliy's face. Gustav and Lena tensed.

Vlad had told them about the people he'd met during the time he'd helped Mae fight the Sorcerer King.

"Don't worry," Delphine said quietly at his faint frown. "She didn't reveal the details of the mission she and Lou Flint undertook in New York. She didn't need to. Most of us in the corps know about the supernatural world that exists alongside ours. After all, we have Immortal DNA inside us."

"Has she allayed your doubts?" Yuliy grunted in the hush that followed.

Vlad hesitated. He could hardly refuse to have Delphine as his bodyguard if she both knew about the otherworldly powers he and Tarang possessed and accepted them.

Still, she doesn't know the whole truth about me. He met the super soldier's gaze squarely, his heartbeat accelerating on a note of apprehension that wasn't him at all. *Here goes nothing.*

"In answer to your prior question, no, I'm not a sorcerer. I am an incubus who possesses demonic magic. And Tarang is my familiar."

Delphine's pupils widened infinitesimally.

"An incubus?" she repeated in a neutral voice.

"My mother was a Fire Witch." Vlad faltered and glanced at Yuliy, guilt twisting his stomach. "And my father is Ilmon, the king of Incubi and Succubi who dwells in Hell."

Yuliy's expression didn't change. His uncle had accepted Ilmon's identity and the truth behind how Vlad came to be conceived with a calmness that still shocked Vlad ever since he'd informed him of what he'd learned in Hell.

He'd wondered what would happen if the crime lord and the demon ever found themselves in the same room. Vlad masked a grimace.

Knowing Ilmon, he'll probably weep buckets and beg for Yuliy's forgiveness.

His father was the biggest crybaby in the underworld, a fact that often worried his demon allies since he had a tendency to drown entire valleys with his tears.

"Shall we get down to business?" Yuliy said curtly. He turned one of his computer monitors around. "Two nights ago, there was an incident in Manhattan. One that will have serious ramifications for this city's criminal underworld if we don't solve it fast."

He pulled up the video that had circulated on the internet before Jared shut it down. "This footage was taken secretly and posted to a public channel. We found the camera hidden inside a plant. It had been shot to pieces."

Vlad's jaw tightened as his uncle played the footage from the *Oro Divino*.

CHAPTER TEN

DELPHINE MAINTAINED A NEUTRAL EXPRESSION AS SHE watched the masked gang break inside the restaurant, Tarang materialize his presence, and Vlad and a man who could only be Enrique Cortes face their enemy in a devastating show of power bathed in gold and crimson magic.

It was her first time seeing the powers Serena had once described. Powers that were as otherworldly as the ones she herself possessed by virtue of the Immortal DNA weaved into her flesh and bones.

She couldn't drag her gaze away from the dazzling sight that was Vlad in action. The way his eyes gleamed with scarlet fire. The diamond blades that sang in his hands. The formidable energy bombs he manifested.

He was a fighter in his prime, as bewitchingly beautiful as he was deadly.

Her pulse quickened at the sight of Vlad crumpling to the floor before the footage ended in a burst of static. The hollow look that flitted across the incubus's face told her he had relived that moment dozens of times.

"This was meant to be a delicate negotiation," Yuliy said in clipped tones as he stopped the video. "The *Black Devils* were brokering a peace deal between the Lucianos and the *Red Dragon* Triad. Instead, the place was attacked by a highly organized team that seemed to know exactly what they were after. Not only that, they disabled all the cameras in and outside the restaurant minutes before the attack."

"They were targeting Vlad," Delphine said.

Vlad flinched. Gustav and Lena exchanged a confused look.

Yuliy narrowed his eyes at Delphine.

"You catch on fast." His tone was laced with admiration.

Delphine studied the crime lord with fresh understanding, the tension coiling through her since the moment she'd stepped foot inside the mansion slowly abating. "That's why you reached out to Gideon. Only a super soldier can protect your nephew right now." She paused. "I believe you hired me to assist with your investigation because I hold insight others might not."

"I can see why you came so highly recommended." Yuliy's gaze shifted to Vlad. "Now, how about you tell us what you've been keeping from me?"

Vlad swallowed, brow furrowing. "Why do you—?"

"Because something is wrong with you and Tarang," Yuliy snapped. "Neither of you have been your normal selves since that night. And Ilya can't meet my eyes for love or money."

Vlad cursed under his breath.

Delphine studied him with a focused look that seemed to see straight through him.

"If they were after your blood, they could have killed you the moment you went down. Why didn't they?"

A muscle jumped in Vlad's jawline. He remained stubbornly silent.

"Killing Vlad would not just mean messing with the *Black Devils*," Yuliy explained in a steely voice. "It would incur the wrath of the *Bratva* syndicate we answer to. There may not be much love lost between us at the best of times, but we protect and avenge our own."

Delphine mulled this over. "So Vlad's death would mean war."

Yuliy dipped his head. "Correct. Which implies they were after something else."

They gazed pointedly at Vlad, Gustav and Lena joining in to frown at the *Black Devils'* heir.

Vlad held their stares mutinously, refusing to give them an answer. Tarang made a soft sound.

Delphine's gaze shifted to the familiar.

The tiger appeared depressed as he laid his head at Vlad's feet.

Just like his master looked when he was trying to forget his troubles last night.

Her mind raced as she connected the pieces of the puzzle she'd been presented with. Super soldiers weren't just renowned for their physical strength. Their intellectual acumen was on a whole other level.

If those men couldn't kill Vlad because it would mean war, then they did something else to him. And the only thing they could do that would take an incubus and his familiar out of the equation is—

The answer came to her with an intuition borne from years of being on the field. Her stomach sank.

"They took your powers." Her gaze bore into Vlad's stiff face. "Or rather, they did something to you and the tiger that means you can't use your magic."

The way Vlad's eyes darkened told her she was right.

Yuliy froze. Lena cursed in Russian.

"Say it isn't so," Gustav mumbled hoarsely in the stunned silence.

Vlad crunched his eyes for a moment before blowing out a heavy sigh and raking his hair with his fingers. "Goddammit!"

The way he tousled his curls reminded Delphine of how she'd sunk her own fingers into his hair last night in the throes of passion. She ignored the heat coiling through her belly and concentrated on the matter at hand.

"So it's true?" Yuliy said in a troubled voice.

Vlad met his uncle's gaze.

"Yes. Tarang and I can't use our powers. I've been cut off from my incubus energy too."

Yuliy curled his hands into fists. "But—how?!"

Vlad hesitated. "Cortes and I sensed a strange kind of magic during the fight. We're pretty certain that's what did it."

Delphine furrowed her brow. "But it didn't affect Cortes or his familiar?"

"Correct," Vlad said bitterly.

She filed that fact away for future analysis.

A muscle jumped in Yuliy's jawline.

"Have you spoken to Mae?" His tone turned harsh. "What about the New York coven?!"

Delphine's ears perked up. *Mae?*

Vlad's face grew pinched. "I can't just run off to the Witch Queen whenever I have a problem. Besides, Cortes and I are pursuing our own line of inquiry."

Yuliy lowered his brows. "This isn't some kind of game, Vlad. Mae Jin is probably the only one who can help you regain your powers." His expression darkened. "Don't tell me you're refusing to seek her help because you still have feelings for her?"

An icy feeling slithered down Delphine's spine at that.

The silence that fell inside the study could have been cut with a knife.

A thunderous look clouded Vlad's face.

"My…*feelings* for Mae have nothing to do with this!" he spat out. "And I'm over her."

"Are you sure?" Yuliy retorted bitterly. "Then why have you been celibate since your war with the Sorcerer King ended?"

Delphine's pulse quickened, the chill in her veins dissipating. She did her best to maintain an impassive expression as she stole a covert glance at Vlad.

Does that mean I'm the first woman he's hooked up with in a while?

"Are you keeping track of my junk, old man?" Vlad growled at his uncle. "Who says I haven't been sleeping around?!"

"Oh, please!" Yuliy scoffed. "Milo would have tattled to our men."

Vlad swore. "I'm going to shoot that guy once he's all

better," he said savagely. "And FYI, I haven't been celibate. I hooked up with someone last night."

Lena almost dropped the teapot. Gustav sucked in air.

Yuliy squinted, like he didn't believe one word of his nephew's claim.

Wariness knotted Delphine's shoulders at the defiant light that dawned in Vlad's eyes.

Please tell me this guy isn't about to—

"I slept with her." Vlad pointed squarely at her.

Tarang made a smug sound, his tail swinging lazily.

Delphine closed her eyes.

Kill me. Kill me now.

She opened them again and found herself the focus of the incubus's triumphant gaze and a battery of shocked stares.

"It was an accident," she said levelly. "A one-night stand. I didn't know who Vlad was and I doubt he knew of my identity either."

Yuliy recovered first.

"I trust whatever happened between you won't compromise this arrangement," he said carefully, his gaze swinging between them.

"It won't," Vlad grunted. "Like she said, it was a one-night stand."

Irritation tightened Delphine's chest for a moment. "He's right. Also, I believe this attack wasn't just about taking Vlad's powers. The timing of it and the leaked footage makes it clear whoever is after him wanted people to see him fail."

The way Vlad's knuckles whitened in his lap told

Delphine her insight had struck uncomfortably close to home again.

Yuliy's face tightened as he absorbed the meaning behind her words.

"The *Black Devils* maintain peace in this city by being the biggest predator in the pond," he said slowly. "And we now have a new role to play as a negotiator between the most influential crime families in New York." His eyes darkened. "Showing weakness, even for a moment—"

"Makes you a target," Delphine finished. "Not only that, it will bring down the reputation of the *Black Devils*, which could be one of their goals." She leveled a sharp gaze at Vlad and Yuliy. "I'm going to need complete access to your security protocols and personnel files, and a detailed layout of all the properties Vlad frequents."

CHAPTER ELEVEN

Despite Vlad's reservations on the matter, Yuliy and Delphine decided that the best place for her to be was at his side twenty-four seven. Which was why he was currently watching the super soldier climb the stairs of his penthouse to one of his guest rooms, a suitcase in hand.

Tarang's tail swished beside him, the tiger's satisfaction humming faintly through their muted connection.

Vlad shot his familiar an accusing look.

"Would it kill you to pretend that this is a problem?" he muttered.

Tarang ignored him and padded toward the kitchen.

Vlad listened to the sound of Delphine settling in upstairs.

He would have offered to take her things up but he suspected the suggestion would have offended her. Delphine in work mode was even more daunting a prospect than she'd been last night.

It made Vlad wonder if all super soldiers were as cold and detached as she was. Though she'd been a fearsome fighter who could easily take down a group of demons, Serena Blake had carried a hint of softness in her eyes and her words.

Then again, she's married and a mother.

Memories of how Delphine had looked last night flitted past his vision and tightened his belly.

The super soldier had been anything but cold in his arms.

What she'd said at the end of their meeting at the mansion brought a faint frown to his face as he headed for the kitchen.

"Whoever came after Vlad knew exactly what he was and how to neutralize him. Which means your enemy has dealings with the criminal underworld *and* the world of magic." The super soldier had paused, as if carefully choosing her next words. "Do you suspect the Lucianos or the *Red Dragon* Triad of being involved in this incident?"

"We've looked into that and we believe the answer is no," Yuliy had replied. "Giovanni and Wei Chen may be good actors but it was clear they feared for their sons' lives that night." He'd pursed his lips. "Still, we'll keep that line of inquiry open."

Vlad was getting stuff ready for lunch when Delphine came downstairs.

"I'm going to sweep the place," she said, strolling to a stop in the archway. "Check entry points, establish secure zones." Her tone was pure professional efficiency. She looked at Tarang. "Will he stay visible to me at all times from now on?"

Tarang stretched languidly from the floor and yawned.

"I think we can take that as a yes," Vlad said drily. He ignored the prickle of awareness coursing down his spine at her steady gaze. "I'm making chicken and bacon Caesar salad. You want some?"

Delphine cut her eyes to the island where he was setting stuff up, interest sparking in her eyes. "I never say no to food."

Vlad couldn't help smiling at that.

Delphine cocked an eyebrow. "What?"

"Nothing." He stepped over to the refrigerator and took out a couple of items for the salad. "It's just that I know someone who has an endless void for a stomach."

"Is it Mae Jin?"

The question made his pulse jump. Vlad's fingers clenched on the refrigerator door for a second before he closed it.

Delphine didn't miss the movement.

He kept his tone deliberately light. "Why do you say that?"

"Your voice changes when you talk about her."

Surprise jolted Vlad once more. No one had ever told him that before.

A sudden stillness came over Delphine. "Are you expecting a visitor?"

Vlad stared, confused by the shift in the conversation. "No."

A gun appeared in her hand faster than he could blink. "Someone's in the elevator."

She moved out into the main corridor, the weapon leveled at his front door in a double-handed grip.

Vlad's heartbeat accelerated. He snatched the handgun secured underneath the island and joined her.

"You can hear the elevator from here?" he said dubiously.

"I have superhuman hearing." Delphine cut her eyes to him. "What are you doing?"

"Helping."

Her eyes narrowed fractionally. "In case you didn't notice, you're the one they're after. Now get behind me."

Vlad's face tightened. "What?"

Delphine's expression grew flinty. "I'm not going to repeat myself, Vlad. Either get behind me or I'll shoot you in the leg."

Vlad's mouth pressed to a thin line. "Is that what a bodyguard is supposed to say to their client?"

"It's what a super soldier says," Delphine retorted coolly. A frown wrinkled her brow. She lowered her gun and slipped it back into the holster at her back. "I don't think it's the enemy." She jerked her chin.

He turned.

Tarang had come out of the kitchen and was sitting in the foyer, his tail sweeping the floor as he faced the door. An impatient sound left the tiger.

Vlad clenched his jaw. Had his incubus powers and their bond been intact, he would have felt his familiar's emotions.

Delphine pulled her cellphone out and tapped the screen a couple of times.

"It's your friend from last night."

Surprise jolted Vlad when she showed him the display. It was live footage from the camera on the landing.

Cortes had just stepped out of the elevator.

"When the hell did you hack into my security system?" Vlad asked, aghast.

Delphine shrugged. "When I was upstairs just now."

The doorbell rang.

"Want me to get that?" the super soldier said.

"No," Vlad ground out. He marched into the foyer and opened the door.

Cortes grinned at him. "Hey."

"What happened to texting?" Vlad said irritably.

"I was in the neighborhood." The Colombian strolled past him, Popo looking around curiously as he hopped down onto Tarang's head. "So, how'd it go with the—" He froze at the sight of Delphine. "Oh."

Popo squawked, equally shocked.

Vlad pinched the bridge of his nose. The last thing he needed right now was a busybody sorcerer and his meddling familiar butting into what was already a complicated situation.

Delphine's gaze found Popo.

"So that's who you were flicking last night," she muttered.

Cortes frowned at his familiar. "Why did you make yourself visible?"

"It was the shock, my Enrique," the parrot said, abashed. "Besides, Tarang says she's a friend." He stepped sideways on the tiger's head and leaned his beak close to his ear. *"Does this mean the incubus got friendzoned by that sexy lady?"* he hissed.

Tarang let out a series of huffs and low growls.

"Oh. Is that right?" Popo straightened and leered at

Vlad and Delphine. "They made sweet, passionate love all night—*ow!*"

Cortes had flicked the bird's beak.

"I can tell you do that often," Delphine said leadenly.

"I have a callus forming on my finger," Cortes muttered. His sharp gaze swung between Delphine and Vlad. "Something tells me you didn't decide to stay over just because you like this guy," he told the super soldier.

"I'm standing right here," Vlad snapped.

"I can see why the two of you get along so well," Delphine said drily.

Cortes arched an eyebrow. "That was a very smart way to avoid my question."

Vlad sighed and rubbed the back of his neck awkwardly. "She's my new bodyguard."

For once, Cortes looked at a loss for words.

"Your bodyguard?" the Colombian said once he'd regained his composure.

"You know, the one Yuliy hired for my protection detail?" Vlad said irritably.

Cortes blinked. He burst out laughing.

Vlad and Delphine frowned as he doubled over.

"Wait!" the Colombian gasped once he could speak again. "So you two hooked up without knowing *you*"—he pointed at Delphine—"would be guarding *him*?!" He indicated Vlad before collapsing into laughter once more.

Popo cackled where he was rolling around on Tarang's head.

"How about we pretend they were the enemy and shoot them?" Vlad growled.

"I'm considering it," Delphine said coolly.

CHAPTER TWELVE

"I still can't believe this." Cortes chortled as he settled at the kitchen island. "Of all the bars in New York, you two had to pick the same one."

"Are you done?" Vlad asked stonily as he plated their lunch.

"For now." The Colombian's gaze sparkled with unholy glee.

"The tiger wants to know if there will be a repeat of last night's passionate performance?" Popo asked cheerfully where he was eating a bowl of dried fruits and nuts next to Tarang.

Tarang grinned around the steak in his mouth.

"One more word and we're having parrot for dinner," Vlad growled, slamming the cutlery drawer closed.

"I can help with that," Delphine said.

"My Enrique!" Popo protested.

"Maybe you should stop commenting on their sex life," Cortes told the familiar drily.

Delphine took the fork Vlad handed her. Their fingers brushed briefly. Heat sparked along her skin at the contact. She did her best to ignore the awareness knotting her belly.

The way Vlad's pupils dilated a little and his mouth tightened told her he'd felt the same thing and was just as determined to steer clear of it.

At least we're on the same page.

"How about we talk about something else?" Cortes's shrewd gaze swung between them. "Like what you discovered at Yuliy's?"

"For one thing, Delphine was given this assignment by Gideon Morgan," Vlad said curtly.

Cortes did a double take. "Gideon Morgan? As in the super soldier mercenary Serena works for?"

"The very one."

Delphine held Cortes's wary stare as she dug into her salad. "Don't tell me you have something against super soldiers too."

"I don't." Cortes glanced at Vlad.

"I don't have anything against super soldiers," Vlad grunted defensively as he straddled a stool.

"Your face said otherwise when we were at your uncle's," Delphine countered mildly.

Irritation darkened Vlad's eyes. "I was just surprised."

Cortes watched their exchange with poorly concealed interest.

"What?" Vlad snapped at the Colombian.

Cortes grinned. "You guys get along pretty well."

Delphine narrowed her eyes fractionally. Vlad's frown deepened.

Cortes ignored their death stares and carried on eating.

"So, any insight as to who was behind the attack and why?"

"Delphine thinks whoever came after me wanted people to see me and the *Black Devils* weakened," Vlad said bitterly. "And by people, she meant the rest of the criminal underworld."

Cortes sobered. "To be fair, that thought did cross my mind. The timing can't be a coincidence." His brow furrowed. "Someone may be trying to destabilize the current power balance in New York."

"I agree," Delphine said levelly. "Our mercenary corps have seen similar patterns in countries where there have been a *coup d'état*."

Vlad hesitated. "That scenario does makes sense."

They ate in silence, each lost to their own thoughts.

Cortes wiped his mouth and put down his napkin at the end of the meal. "Speaking of power balance, I've heard some strange rumors about Wei Chen's Kingston contacts."

Vlad frowned as he got up and cleared their plates. "What kind of rumors?"

"The kind that make seasoned criminals nervous." Cortes drummed his fingers on the counter. "They're involved in some pretty nasty stuff."

Delphine was pondering how much nastier the criminal underworld could get when the Colombian's phone rang.

Cortes stiffened when he checked the screen. "It's one of the guys watching Mrs. Son-Ha's place." He took the call. Whatever he heard made his expression brighten. "How long ago?" He listened for another moment. "Keep an eye on the house and make sure she doesn't leave. Block the street if you have to."

Unease prickled Delphine's scalp.

Vlad had reluctantly admitted exactly what line of inquiry he and Cortes were pursuing to her and Yuliy that morning. The fact that it involved a Shaman who could see spirits had done little to reassure her. Even though she knew there were things in this world that could not be explained by logic or science, the super soldier inside her drew a line at ghosts.

"Mrs. Son-Ha is back?" Vlad asked when Cortes ended the call, hope underscoring his voice.

"She just got home. Looks like she's been away. My guy said she had a case."

"Finally." Vlad turned to exit the kitchen. "Let's go."

"Hold up," Delphine said. Her tone stopped the incubus mid-stride. "We need a plan of action first."

"The plan of action is to go see Mrs. Son-Ha," Vlad said impatiently.

"I get that you want to talk to this woman, but everything you do from now on needs to be carefully thought out. You're currently without your powers and someone strong enough to suppress them is still out there."

Vlad bristled. "I can handle myself."

Delphine arched an eyebrow. "Like you handled yourself at the *Oro Divino*?"

Cortes winced. "Ouch. She kinda has a point."

"Tarang and Cortes will be with us," Vlad said flintily.

Cortes lifted his hands. "Hey, don't bring me into your lovers' spat."

Delphine's eyes shrank to slits. "This is not a lovers' spat."

"Yeah," Vlad snapped. "Whose side are you on, anyway?"

"The one that entertains me the most," Cortes said bluntly. This earned him a pair of heavy frowns. He sighed. "How about you listen to your super soldier bodyguard?"

A muscle worked in Vlad's cheek. He finally relented. "What do you suggest?"

She took out her phone, mapped out the two most defensible approaches to Mrs. Son-Ha's address as well as three viable exit routes, and showed them her plan.

"Can you have your men cover the property while we're inside?" she asked Vlad and Cortes.

"We don't need to," Vlad said. "There's a divine barrier protecting the place. If anyone with magic or demonic powers tries to attack, it will repel them."

Delphine gave them a skeptical look. "A divine barrier?"

Cortes grimaced. "You'll see what we mean when we get there."

"We should be able to take care of anyone else who turns up," Vlad said, heading into the foyer. "I can fight."

Delphine frowned. "We should have your guards follow us anyway."

Vlad grudgingly agreed.

She made the call and coordinated their backup on the ride in the elevator. Tarang padded silently beside them when they stepped out into the underground garage.

Vlad pressed his remote key. The Bentley's lights flashed.

"We should take my wheels." Delphine indicated the Range Rover parked beside his convertible.

"Why?" Vlad said.

Delphine counted to three in her head. "Because Gideon modified it to be literally tank proof."

Vlad stared. "Did you just grind your teeth?"

Cortes made a strangled sound.

"And why do we need a tank-proof vehicle?" Vlad added suspiciously.

Delphine ignored the silently laughing Colombian and did her best not to scowl at the incubus.

"I did not grind my teeth. As for your second question, it's because there are people out there who want your blood and wouldn't give a rat's ass about ramming your precious Bentley into a river."

Vlad pursed his lips. "You just did it again. You ground your teeth."

Delphine's fingers twitched. "Maybe it's because my client is turning out to be a royal asshole and I'm seriously considering putting a bullet through his leg," she snapped.

Vlad blinked. Tarang huffed worriedly.

Cortes turned away slightly, shoulders quivering. Popo's gaze swung avidly between Vlad and Delphine.

"Technically, Yuliy is your client," Vlad murmured.

"Dude," Cortes choked out.

Delphine counted to five this time.

"Are we doing this or are we going to stand here having a debate?" she said glacially.

Vlad watched her for a moment before sighing. "Alright, we'll take the Range Rover."

"Cortes will ride shotgun," Delphine said briskly. "You're in the back."

"It's broad daylight," the incubus protested. "It's not like we're storming a fortress."

"No." Delphine opened the back door and indicated the interior. "We're protecting a vulnerable asset."

The way Vlad's eyes darkened told her she'd hurt his pride.

"Fine!" He stormed over to the vehicle, got inside, and slammed the door shut after Tarang climbed in.

Delphine lowered her brows.

"Any chance that magic made him regress to a petulant teenager?" she asked Cortes.

The Colombian laughed.

The ride to Glendale took place with a surprising lack of mishaps. Delphine stayed alert as she turned the Range Rover into a quiet cul-de-sac lined with bare trees, the *Black Devils* guards following at a distance. She parked behind an ancient Subaru at the end of the road and stared at the two-story clapboard house to the right.

It was a deceptively normal-looking home with a neat yard full of garden gnomes.

Delphine picked out Cortes's men loitering inside two SUVs that stood out like sore thumbs where they were stationed amidst the weathered vehicles hedging the curbs.

"Your guys should hire a beat-up Chevy next time they

do a stakeout," she told Cortes as they stepped out of the Range Rover.

The Colombian grimaced. "That might hurt their pride."

Vlad alighted from the vehicle with Tarang, his expression tense.

Tension oozed through Delphine when they crossed the front yard to a redbrick porch. Something had brushed against her senses. Something that made her skin prickle with an otherworldly awareness.

Cortes clocked her expression. "That's the barrier we were telling you about. It feels kinda creepy at first."

Delphine masked a grimace. Creepy didn't even begin to describe it.

"We do this my way," she said. "I'll go in first and clear the place before you guys enter. At the first sign of trouble—"

A chorus of excited barks and yips erupted from the property.

"Too late," Cortes muttered.

The front door opened.

An elderly Korean woman in a neon purple tracksuit stood in the hallway, a scowl on her face.

"Are you kids going to stand out there all day? The spirits are getting impatient."

The Chihuahua in her arms wriggled excitedly at the sight of Tarang and Popo.

CHAPTER THIRTEEN

Vlad and Cortes greeted Mrs. Son-Ha and her dog Dexter. A small black-and-tan Shih Tzu poked his head around the old lady's legs and yapped at them.

"Pipe down," Mrs. Son-Ha told the Shih Tzu sharply. "It's not like this is your first time seeing the tiger and the pervert bird."

Popo puffed his chest out proudly at that. Cortes rolled his eyes.

The Shih Tzu issued one final yip before whirling around and disappearing down the passage to the living room. She poked her head out again, a pair of Chihuahuas, another two Shih Tzus, and a dog whose breed Vlad had yet to determine joining her in her curious perusal of their visitors.

Mrs. Son-Ha squinted. "Well? Are you coming in or not?"

Delphine took the lead when they entered the house. Mrs. Son-Ha didn't miss the move.

"Who's the pretty lady?" she asked as they divested themselves of their coats and shoes, Delphine following Vlad and Cortes's example.

"My new bodyguard," Vlad admitted reluctantly.

Delphine dipped her chin curtly at the Shaman. "Delphine Dubois."

Mrs. Son-Ha's gaze flitted from Delphine to Vlad. Her expression turned shrewd. "I see."

Vlad decided not to ask her what she meant by that.

The amused gleam in Cortes's eyes had him swallowing a groan.

It was bad enough being ferried around by Delphine. Having the Columbian witness his fall from grace wasn't helping the situation.

"My spirits are quite taken with you," Mrs. Son-Ha said. Curiosity sparkled in her eyes as she observed Delphine. "They can sense a hint of divine energy coming from your soul."

Delphine's shoulders knotted fractionally. "What do you mean?"

Mrs. Son-Ha cocked her head. "You're one of them super soldiers, aren't you?"

Delphine narrowed her eyes with an expression that probably made a lot of people quake in their boots. "You know about super soldiers?"

Mrs. Son-Ha waved a vague hand, clearly unimpressed by her threatening stare. "I heard about that Serena chick. And I know about Immortals. You smell a little like one." She paused. "You also smell of something alien. Something…not quite natural."

Delphine hesitated.

"That would be my nanorobots," she admitted grudgingly.

"Oh. Is that so?" Mrs. Son-Ha's gaze switched to Vlad. She grimaced. "As for you, that's a hell of a nasty curse you've got on you."

Vlad's pulse jumped. He exchanged a startled look with Cortes and Delphine.

"I've got a curse on me?" he asked, mouth dry.

His mind raced. Though people assumed sorcerers and witches used curses all the time, they weren't something routinely encountered in the world of magic.

"Not just you." Mrs. Son-Ha eyeballed Tarang. "The tiger's been cursed too."

Tarang made a worried sound and pressed against Vlad's leg.

Mrs. Son-Ha turned and headed down the passage. "Let's go to the kitchen. I'll make you kids some hot cocoa."

"We're a bit old for hot—" Delphine started.

Mrs. Son-Ha stopped and squinted at the super soldier over her shoulder. "You're gonna drink the hot cocoa and you're gonna enjoy it, missy."

"Yes, ma'am," Delphine responded automatically.

She blinked in the next instant, surprised.

Cortes patted her shoulder. "You get used to it. We think she was a drill sergeant in her other life."

They followed Mrs. Son-Ha to a cozy back kitchen that smelled of incense and ginseng tea. Tiny bells hung from the ceiling here and there, their gentle chimes causing wariness to creep onto Delphine's face as she took a seat at the kitchen table.

Vlad sympathized with her discomfort. The Shaman's place had an eldritch vibe that would make even the Pope jumpy.

Mrs. Son-Ha flicked a light switch and put the kettle on.

Steaming cups of hot cocoa appeared in front of them a moment later.

Their host took the chair at the head of the table.

"So what the heck did you do to get yourself cursed?" she asked Vlad sharply.

Vlad hesitated before giving her an account of what had taken place at the *Oro Divino* three nights ago.

"A peace deal?" the old woman repeated with a frown.

"Yes. We never completed the negotiations." The words had barely left Vlad's mouth when he stiffened.

"That's another factor we failed to consider," Delphine said with a faint frown.

"These people may not just be after you and the *Black Devils*." Cortes lowered his brows. "They may very well not want this peace deal to go through in the first place."

Vlad's heart thumped against his ribs.

Why didn't I think of that? If that's the case, then the Lucianos and Wei Chen really are innocent.

Mrs. Son-Ha rose and came over to him. "Strip."

Tarang's eyes rounded. Popo sucked in air.

"What?" Vlad said hoarsely.

"I need to examine your core," Mrs. Son-Ha said impatiently.

Vlad swallowed, his gaze darting to a shocked Cortes and a poker-faced Delphine. "And I have to be naked for this?"

"Who said anything about being naked?" Mrs. Son-Ha said irritably. "I just need you to open your shirt."

"Oh." Heat crawled up Vlad's neck at the amused glint in Delphine's eyes. He shrugged out of his jacket, undid his tie, and flipped his shirt buttons open.

Mrs. Son-Ha dragged a chair over and sat opposite him.

"This might sting a little," she muttered.

She leaned in and pressed her hand against his stomach.

Vlad tensed at her cool touch. Nothing happened.

The light flickered, causing Cortes and Delphine to glance uneasily at the ceiling. Glass trembled on the shelves.

The hairs rose on the back of Vlad's neck when Mrs. Son-Ha's pupils glowed white.

The same pale light came to life around her fingertips.

Heat flared on his skin, causing his breath to catch. He clenched his teeth when the sensation turned into a sharp, prickling feeling.

Tarang began pacing the floor beside them, little huffs of concern leaving his throat.

Mrs. Son-Ha frowned after several seconds. She lifted her hand off Vlad's abdomen and sat back, the radiance fading from her hand and pupils.

"That's a voodoo spell."

"Voodoo?" Cortes's eyes widened. "You mean like—"

"Traditional African sorcery?" Mrs. Son-Ha shook her head, her expression grim. "This is much older. Much darker. It shares some characteristics with black magic but it's also different." She studied Vlad. "Someone bound your powers using their own blood. Like I said, it's a nasty curse."

Realization dawned on Delphine's face. She looked at Cortes.

"That's why the spell didn't affect you and your familiar. It was meant only for Vlad."

Vlad's throat tightened as he held their host's gaze. "Can you undo it?"

Mrs. Son-Ha reluctantly shook her head. "I'm a Shaman, not a witch. There are only two ways I can think of to remove this spell from your core and that of your tiger. Either you force the sorcerer whose work this is to undo it. Or you kill him." She paused. "The third way is to find the objects he used his blood on to transfer the spell to you."

"Objects?" Cortes repeated.

"You mean dolls?" Delphine said skeptically.

Mrs. Son-Ha bobbed her head.

Shit. Blood pounded dully in Vlad's head in the hush that followed.

"What about Mae?" He met Mrs. Son-Ha's gaze. "Could she undo the curse?"

"Possibly." The Shaman lowered her brows. "Your core may need fixing afterward though, like Cortes's did."

"We should call her," the Colombian told Vlad in a worried voice.

"I concur," Delphine said.

Something in her tone had him looking over at her.

Her eyes were dark with a nameless emotion.

"There's something else you need to know," Mrs. Son-

Ha warned. "This curse will become permanent in about forty-eight hours."

Ice filled Vlad's veins. "What?!"

Tarang let out a distressed yowl that set the dogs barking.

Mrs. Son-Ha reached over and patted the tiger, her expression full of disquiet for the first time since they'd entered her house. "I would call Mae sooner rather than later."

But trying to get in touch with the Witch Queen proved to be a fruitless exercise.

Vlad stared at his phone in the back of the Range Rover, Mae's number glowing on the screen as he hit redial for what felt like the hundredth time. The call went straight to voicemail, just like every other attempt he'd made in the fifteen minutes since they'd left Glendale.

Frustration churned his stomach.

Where the hell is she?!

Delphine's gaze met his briefly in the rearview mirror of the Range Rover. Though her expression remained neutral, he detected concern in the slight tightening of her mouth.

They were working against the clock and they all knew it.

"I can't get through to Bryony either," Cortes said stiffly, his phone in hand and Popo uncharacteristically quiet on his shoulder.

Delphine frowned and glanced at them. "Want me to drive over there? I know the address."

Vlad swallowed and dipped his head.

Hopefully, someone in the New York coven will know Mae's

whereabouts. His stomach sank when another thought followed. *If she's in Europe, it might take her more than a day to get back here.*

Delphine had just pulled onto the Long Island Expressway when tension tightened her shoulders. Her gaze flicked from the wing mirrors to the rearview mirror and back again.

"We've got company."

Cortes looked behind them, a gun appearing in his hand. "How many?"

Vlad scowled and twisted around.

"Three vehicles. I think they've been shadowing us since Ridgewood," Delphine said calmly. "Black SUV at our six. Silver sedan two cars back on the left. Dark blue van that keeps going in and out of sight."

"Got them," Cortes said coldly.

"Great," Vlad muttered darkly. "Just what we need."

He removed the weapon in the small of his back and checked it. Tarang let out a low growl beside him.

"This might be the fallout Yuliy and you were worried about," Delphine told him curtly.

Vlad exchanged a troubled look with Cortes.

A rival gang out to kill the *Black Devils*' heir made sense right now.

Delphine dialed the guards following them and updated them on the situation.

"Drop back and stay on that van's six," she told the driver coolly. "We're taking a detour."

Vlad gasped when she floored the gas pedal, twisted the steering wheel, and cut across two lanes toward an exit.

CHAPTER FOURTEEN

Cortes grunted as he slammed into the door, his hand rising to protect Popo. The sound of honking horns followed in the Range Rover's wake.

So did the vehicles tailing them.

Delphine barreled down a service road running parallel to Newtown Creek. Her hands tightened fractionally on the steering wheel when she glanced at their pursuers in the side mirrors.

"They knew our route."

She didn't have to look at Cortes and Vlad to sense their scowls.

The implications of her words hung heavily in the air.

"You think someone leaked our location?" Vlad said.

"Either that or they're following us via a satcom."

She lifted her foot off the gas pedal as she crossed a couple of junctions, allowing the vehicles on their tail to close in on them. Tarang's growl vibrated through the

Range Rover, the tiger's hackles rising as he sensed the approaching threat.

Delphine spotted what she was looking for, yanked the wheel hard to the right, and sent the Range Rover skidding into an alley that led in the direction of the docks. Engines roared behind them, their pursuers abandoning any pretense of subtlety as they gave chase.

A bullet pinged against the rear bumper.

Delphine hit the window control, pulled her gun out, and fired back, one hand holding the steering wheel firmly and her gaze focused on the road ahead.

The shot cracked the windshield of the black SUV. It slowed.

"That got their attention," Cortes muttered.

Delphine raised the window back up and hit the dial button on her phone.

The driver of the *Black Devils'* SUV answered on the first ring.

"Get rid of the van," she ordered. "Keep at least one man alive if you can."

Gunfire erupted behind them as Vlad's guards began shooting at the enemy.

Delphine accelerated and weaved the Range Rover between buildings and abandoned shipping containers.

Vlad glanced warily at their increasingly deserted surroundings. "Where are we headed?"

"Somewhere I spotted on the satellite map before we left your place." She met his gaze in the rearview mirror. "Better to choose our battleground than let them choose it for us."

Vlad nodded, something that looked a little like relief flitting in his eyes.

Delphine ignored the way her chest tightened at this display of trust. She knew it wasn't easy for the incubus to surrender control in any situation, let alone a combat one where he normally excelled. The fact that he was willing to put his life in her hands made her feel things she shouldn't be feeling about a client.

But now was not the time to mull over her confusing emotions.

She took another sharp turn and saw her target.

"Up ahead. Warehouse on the left with the loading dock. It has plenty of cover and multiple exit routes in case we need one."

Vlad steadied his hands on the door and the roof. "Go for it!"

Cortes clenched his jaw and braced against the dashboard.

Delphine barely slowed as she swung the Range Rover sideways, using their momentum to slide them into the warehouse and between two rows of containers. She slammed the brakes and switched off the engine.

The move would buy them fifteen seconds, twenty at most.

It was more than enough for what she needed to do.

Delphine exited the vehicle and circled to the rear, Vlad and Cortes following. She popped the trunk and withdrew two vests.

They looked like standard tactical gear. Except body armor didn't shimmer like it had a life of its own.

She tossed them at Vlad and Cortes.

"Put these on. They're nanorobot vests. They will stop pretty much anything except for a tank."

Cortes made a face as he shrugged into his. "You know, you people have an unhealthy obsession with tanks."

"You try and be in a war zone where your enemy is actively trying to flatten you with one," Delphine muttered.

Tires screeched somewhere outside. The sound of doors opening and slamming shut came next.

Delphine's pulse quickened. *Ten seconds.*

Tarang growled softly beside Vlad. The incubus hastily slipped his vest on and accepted the extra magazines she handed to him and Cortes.

Voices reached them as the men outside began exploring the area.

They crouched wordlessly behind the Range Rover. Tarang and Popo grew still.

"Wait until the last minute to use your magic," Delphine told Cortes in a low voice. "It will give away our position otherwise."

The Colombian nodded grimly.

The pursuers' footsteps grew close.

"They can't have gone far," someone said as they entered the warehouse. "They have to be hiding around here somewhere, like the rats that they are."

Another man chuckled at that.

Delphine heard Vlad grind his teeth.

Armed figures appeared in a gap between the containers.

She counted nine men.

That's five guys in one vehicle and four in another. She narrowed her eyes. *Which means the* Black Devils *either took the van out or are still engaged with them.*

Delphine signaled the number to Vlad and Cortes and motioned at them to follow her. They twisted and fell into her steps as she circled quietly around them.

She guided them to a junction between the containers and pointed. Vlad and Cortes exchanged a wary glance before dipping their heads.

They separated and headed for the rungs in the walls of the containers she'd indicated.

In warfare, a higher vantage point was always better than a lower one.

Tarang's muscles bunched as he prepared to leap. The tiger jumped with fluid grace and landed atop the metal box Vlad had climbed with the faintest thump.

The sound made their enemy pause where they'd been searching the warehouse.

"You guys hear that?" someone said tensely.

Delphine scaled the container she'd chosen as her shooting platform and rolled silently across the surface to the edge. She stopped, braced her elbows, and gripped her gun tightly.

Her shots brought down two men before they could react.

Vlad and Cortes fired, taking out another couple of armed figures.

The remaining men dove for cover.

The way the shots echoed around the warehouse

meant it took a moment for their attackers to pinpoint where they had come from. Delphine eliminated another guy while they were still looking.

"Over there! On top of those containers!" someone yelled.

Sparks erupted as bullets slammed into the walls of the metal boxes, the enemy converging swiftly on their location.

Delphine stayed low, as did Vlad and Cortes. She clenched her jaw.

There goes half our advantage.

The hairs rose on the back of her neck. She twisted sharply.

The shot that would have bored a hole into her head pierced metal an inch from her shoulder.

"Vlad, Cortes! Three o'clock high!" Delphine barked.

She cursed and moved as more bullets rained down around her.

The incubus's and the Colombian's heads snapped around, their gazes finding the armed figure on the gantry thirty feet above them. The man's aim shifted to Vlad.

Vlad rolled as metal pinged next to him. He grunted when a shot slammed into his nanorobot vest and crumpled on contact.

Gold exploded in Cortes's and Popo's eyes, their magic washing across Delphine's skin on a warm wave. A whip appeared in the sorcerer's hand. Popo rose as he snapped the weapon, the cord extending impossibly high.

The figure on the gantry cursed when it wrapped around his ankle. He flailed wildly, his vision obstructed by the parrot pecking at his head. Cortes yanked hard and brought him to the ground in a sickening thud of smashing bones while Delphine and Vlad took out two more armed figures on the main floor.

Her stomach dropped.

Where are the other two?!

Tarang's roar shook the air as he leapt from the container.

The men who'd circled behind them cried out when the familiar's shadow engulfed them. Delphine grimaced as the sounds turned into wet gurgles.

The tiger might not be able to use his magic, but there was nothing wrong with his fangs and claws.

Her heart thundered against her ribs as she rose to her feet.

Less than five minutes after they were ambushed inside the warehouse, the fight was over.

She jumped down from the container, walked over to where Tarang loomed threateningly over the man who'd survived his attack, and kicked his gun out of reach.

Cortes dropped lightly to the ground and followed the sound of groaning into the main area of the warehouse. The only other survivor swore when the sorcerer stepped on the hand he was using to weakly lift a gun. Cortes leveled the muzzle of his firearm at the enemy's skull, his expression icy.

Popo landed on his shoulder with a threatening squawk.

Motion near the entrance caught Delphine's eye as she joined the sorcerer. She swung her gun around in a double-handed grip, her aim rock steady.

"Woah!" The *Black Devils* guard who'd entered the building froze and raised his hands defensively.

Delphine relaxed a fraction. It was the driver she'd been talking with.

She holstered her weapon as the rest of Vlad's men appeared.

"You got rid of the van?"

The guard grimaced. "We did. But they're all dead."

"We got a couple of survivors." Delphine looked down at the tiger who'd appeared beside her. "Although I'm not sure how long the guy he took down will last."

Tarang made a pleased sound and rubbed against her leg.

Delphine's scalp prickled. "Where's your master?"

The familiar huffed, his tail drooping a little.

Delphine twisted on her heels, her chest tight with dread. "Vlad?!"

"I'm here," the incubus said from somewhere atop the container.

Relief loosened the knot in her belly. "Why aren't you coming down?"

Cortes looked equally puzzled as he joined her, the *Black Devils* taking charge of the attacker he'd pinned down.

"I have a situation."

Concern quickened Delphine's pulse once more. She took a couple of steps forward. "Are you hurt?!"

There was a moment's hesitation.

"Don't laugh," Vlad warned.

Delphine and Cortes exchanged a confused frown.

A heavy sigh came from the top of the container. "I got shot in the ass."

Delphine blinked. She bit her lip hard.

Cortes's face crumpled. He twisted on his heels, his shoulders quaking as he tried to muffle his snorts.

A couple of the *Black Devils* men made choked sounds.

"I can hear you guys laughing!" Vlad snarled.

CHAPTER FIFTEEN

"Stop squirming," the healer muttered.

"I'm not squirming," Vlad grumbled. He was lying face down on an examination table in the New York coven's infirmary, butt exposed to the elements and dignity in tatters. "I'm expressing my discomfort in a manly way."

"You're squirming," Delphine drawled from where she leaned against the wall, arms crossed.

Though her expression remained solemn, Vlad could tell she was grinning inside.

He scowled. "I got shot in the ass. I think I'm entitled to some squirming."

Tarang made a worried sound next to the table.

The healer, a middle-aged witch with steel-gray hair and zero patience for his complaints, prodded the wound with glowing green fingers. "The bullet went clean through. You're lucky the guy didn't aim any lower or it would have—you know."

"Emasculated him?" Cortes contributed, struggling to keep a straight face.

Popo snickered on his shoulder.

"I was gonna say blow one of his balls clean off, but that works too," the witch grunted. Her familiar, a stoat, squealed softly on her shoulder.

Vlad cut his eyes to Cortes. "How about you step outside? I'm barely hanging on to the shreds of my modesty as it is."

"Heck no," Cortes chuckled. "I need to immortalize this moment for Mae and Nikolai."

To Vlad's relief, the familiar twinge that should have clenched his heart failed to manifest at the mention of the Witch Queen's name.

"If you dare take a picture, I'll tell Anya what happened in that strip club we went to for that Christmas party with the *Black Devils*," he growled at Cortes.

The Colombian's expression fell. "Dude, that's low even for you."

"What'd you do?" Delphine asked.

Cortes sighed. "Something no man should ever do to a dancing pole. In my defense, I was exceptionally drunk that night."

"You were fabulous, my Enrique," Popo gushed. "No one could look as good as you sliding and grinding—"

"Shut up, Bird Brain," Cortes snapped.

"How much longer?" Vlad asked the healer between gritted teeth.

"There, all done," the witch said brightly. "I'd suggest you avoid sitting for the next few hours."

"Great," Vlad said sourly, yanking his trousers up. "I'll just hover."

"We have a doughnut ring somewhere," the witch said helpfully. "Would you like me to fetch—?"

"No!"

"Is he always this cranky?" the witch asked Delphine and Cortes.

A faint smile tugged at the corners of the super soldier's mouth. "He has his moments."

Vlad knew from the way her gaze skimmed his body exactly what she was thinking about. Heat coiled through his gut despite himself.

The infirmary door opened. Bryony swept in, her familiar Penley at her heels. The High Priestess stopped and watched as Vlad carefully slid off the couch.

She raised an eyebrow. "You really got shot in the ass?"

"No comment." The incubus adjusted his outfit with as much dignity as he could muster. "Have you heard from Mae? We've been trying to ring her."

Bryony's face clouded over. "You can't reach her either?"

Vlad's heart sank at her words. He could tell she wasn't lying.

If anything, the High Priestess looked worried.

"That's not like her." Cortes furrowed his brow. "Did something happen in Europe?"

"Not that we know of." Bryony hesitated. "Although, Abraham does have a theory."

Abraham Whitworth, Bryony's aide, elaborated on his speculation in the High Priestess's office minutes later.

"They're probably shacked up somewhere," the

sorcerer said with an utter lack of concern as he served them tea.

"Ah." Cortes made a face.

Vlad scowled.

Abraham shrugged at his expression. "They're a young couple in love. They're visiting another country. It's bound to happen." He waved a hand. "One minute you're admiring St. Peter's Basilica, the next minute you're getting hot and heavy in the gardens of the Colosseum."

Bryony pursed her lips. "Mae did say Nikolai's stamina was something else."

Vlad pinched the bridge of his nose and muttered something rude under his breath.

"By the way, who's your lady friend?" Abraham jerked his head at Delphine where she stood to attention next to the door.

"She's my new bodyguard," the incubus said reluctantly.

"What happened to Ilya and Milo?" Bryony asked.

Vlad sighed. "It's a long story." He made the introductions.

Bryony brightened. "You're a friend of Serena's?"

"Yes, I am," Delphine replied carefully.

"Don't just stand there." The High Priestess waved her over. "Come, sit with us."

The super soldier hesitated before crossing the room and taking the seat that would give her first sight of anyone approaching the office, a move no one commented on. A crunching sound had her looking around.

Tarang was munching happily on the platter of steak the coven chef had sent up for him.

"The tiger looks like he's made himself right at home," Delphine remarked.

Abraham grimaced. "At least Tarang has manners. If Brimstone and Hellreaver were here, I'd been scraping flecks of meat off the bookshelves for days."

Tarang huffed smugly.

"Why are you looking for Mae?" Bryony asked Vlad curiously. "It sounds like it's something serious."

Vlad and Cortes exchanged a guarded glance before telling the witch and her aide about the incident at the *Oro Divino* and what Mrs. Son-Ha had revealed to them in Glendale that afternoon.

"Wait." Bryony stared. "You're under a *voodoo curse*?!"

"And you have less than forty-eight hours to break it?" Abraham said, pale-faced.

"Yeah." Vlad ran a hand tiredly through his hair, the events of the day finally catching up to him. "Although I would rather not rely on Mae, I was hoping she might be able to undo it."

A strained hush descended on the room.

Bryony drummed her fingers on her arm rest, her expression focused. "Since we can't get in touch with her, we'll have to find another solution."

Vlad blinked. "Are you sure you want to get involved in this?"

Bryony scowled. "Of course we do. You are one of our people."

Warmth filled Vlad's chest at the witch's words. He'd

always assumed the only people he could count on were Yuliy and the *Black Devils*. Now he had Mae, Nikolai, Cortes, and a whole other bunch of witches and sorcerers he could rely upon.

And a super soldier or two. Vlad's gaze flicked to Delphine.

"Abraham, see if any of our contacts can shed some light on that curse," Bryony said briskly. She studied Vlad with a frown. "In the meantime, I might know a thing or two that can help you track down the sorcerer who did this to you."

Vlad's pulse accelerated. Delphine straightened in her seat.

"The kind of voodoo magic Mrs. Son-Ha described requires three things: the sorcerer's blood, dolls of the targets of the curse, and proximity."

Delphine narrowed her eyes. "Proximity?"

Bryony dipped her head. "For this particular curse to work, the dolls have to be near the victim. And the caster needs to be close by when he invokes the curse."

"How close?" Delphine asked in a deadly voice.

Bryony's mouth flattened to a thin line. "From the accounts I recall, within thirty to forty feet."

Vlad clenched his jaw. He looked at Cortes. "So he was either in the room with us or—"

"Somewhere in the building," Cortes finished with a dark look. "There's something we haven't talked about. The Kingston connections Wei Chen mentioned. Voodoo is popular in that part of the world."

Vlad's fists tightened on his lap. *He's right.*

"We should go take a look at the restaurant," Delphine told Vlad curtly. "And I'll need a copy of that leaked video footage and any other security recordings you have of the building in the past month. They've been planning this for some time."

CHAPTER SIXTEEN

JARED CALLED VLAD ON THE DRIVE TO THE RESTAURANT.

"Special Affairs and NYPD have completed their forensic examination of the *Oro Divino*."

Vlad's shoulders knotted. "You guys find anything I should know about?"

"If you mean clues about the magic that incapacitated you, no." The Immortal hesitated. "You know I can't reveal details about the ongoing investigation. How about you and Cortes? You come up with anything on your end?"

"Yeah. We found out I was cursed."

Jared inhaled sharply. "What?!"

"We went to see Mrs. Son-Ha," Vlad said bitterly. "Tarang and I are under the effect of a voodoo curse. And we have less than two days to reverse it before it becomes permanent."

The Immortal was silent for a moment.

"This is not directly related to the investigation about

the *Oro Divino* incident, so I guess there's no harm in telling you," he said in a guarded voice. "A friend of mine just turned up in town. He's with the DEA. There are some people of interest to them in the city right now."

Vlad straightened in the back seat of the Range Rover, conscious of Delphine's frowning glance in the rearview mirror. "Any of them from Kingston by any chance?"

"I see you already know about them."

"Not the details. Giovanni mentioned he wasn't happy about Wei Chen's new Kingston contacts during the peace talk. It caught my and Cortes's attention." Vlad frowned. "We know some of the bigger Caribbean gangs have been desperate to establish a trading route on the East Coast."

"You think Wei Chen is trying to facilitate that here?" Jared said stiffly.

"She knows better than to cut a deal with them without informing our *Bratva*." Vlad dropped his head against the backrest, suddenly exhausted. "It could be that they're using her."

"That woman is too clever to be fooled by some snot-nosed kids from Jamaica," Jared muttered.

"You're right." Vlad sighed and rubbed his temple.

"By the way, you wouldn't happen to know anything about a shoot-out in Newtown Creek earlier today, would you?" the Immortal grunted.

"No," Vlad lied.

They'd since found out that the gang who'd attacked them that afternoon was a newly formed Peruvian syndicate that had been making noise for all the wrong reasons in the past year. Their boss was currently on his way to Yuliy's estate to explain exactly why his son had sent his men after Vlad.

Jared sighed, not buying the lie for one second. "Just make sure you guys keep the body count to a minimum while you resolve this mess."

❄

THE *ORO DIVINO* WAS EERILY QUIET WHEN THEY ARRIVED. The maitre d'hotel greeted them at the service entrance.

"The insurance adjusters were here this morning," he told Vlad as they crossed the main kitchen area. "I've kept the third floor sealed off, as you requested."

The stench of gunpowder still lingered in the private dining room three days after the attack. The smell registered on Delphine's radar the moment she crossed the threshold, her nanorobots ten times more sensitive than a human nose.

Her gaze swept the space.

Bullet holes peppered the walls like deadly constellations. The overturned table in the middle of the floor bore deep scars from where projectiles had struck its reinforced surface.

Though the cleaning crew had done a decent job of clearing up most of the debris, glass still crunched underfoot as she crossed the room, noting details she'd missed in the grainy footage she'd watched at Yuliy's mansion. She did a full circuit before retracing her steps, Vlad and Cortes watching her.

Delphine stopped and crouched to examine a spent casing half-hidden under a chair.

"They knew exactly where to breach and how to funnel the targets." She looked around the room, tracking invisible angles only her mind could see. "And they knew where everyone would be sitting."

Tension knotted Vlad's shoulders.

"The table arrangement was only finalized the morning of the meeting."

"They must have had someone on the inside feeding them information in real time," Cortes concluded with a grim expression.

Delphine rose and headed for an ornate potted plant by the window.

"Is this where your men found the camera?"

Vlad approached. "Yes."

Delphine studied the mounting point and angle.

"High-end equipment. Wireless. Remote activated." She frowned. "They wanted footage of what happened to you specifically."

"To confirm the curse worked?"

She met his gaze. "And to prove that the *Black Devils'* heir could be taken down."

Vlad's jaw tightened.

Delphine suppressed the urge to reach out and stroke his cheek.

"I need to see your personnel files," she said curtly. "Everyone who's had access to this floor in the last four to six weeks."

"I'll talk to Antonio."

The maitre d'hotel was efficient, producing the necessary records within the hour.

But it was the security footage from the cameras in and around the restaurant that demanded their attention as night fell. They ended up in Vlad's penthouse, surrounded by takeout containers and three laptops showing multiple camera feeds.

"This is pointless," Vlad muttered around midnight, rubbing his eyes. "We've been through the video from the night of the attack and the ones from the days preceding it like a dozen times already."

Cortes had left. He had an early appointment the next day and had promised to catch up with them late morning.

"Sometimes what matters is what happened before," Delphine murmured, her eyes never leaving the screens. "The setup. The preparation. That's where perpetrators often leave a clue."

She was acutely aware of the incubus on the couch beside her, close enough that she could feel his warmth. The attraction that had sparked to life between them that first night still simmered under her skin.

Delphine reminded herself once again that there was a good reason people never mixed business with pleasure.

Vlad's head started nodding around two a.m.

"Get some sleep," she told him. "I've got this."

"You should get some rest too." He blinked and scrubbed a hand down his face.

"I'm a super soldier." She allowed a faint smile to curve her lips. "I can go days without sleep."

Vlad was already drifting off. Tarang curled protectively at the incubus's feet as his breathing evened out. The tiger kept her company as she worked through the night, his gleaming eyes on the monitors she was watching.

Delphine got up to stretch and make herself a coffee at around four a.m., only to find Tarang had followed her into the kitchen.

She looked down. "Aren't you supposed to be watching over your master?"

The tiger issued a friendly rumble and leaned heavily against her leg.

She gave him a steak as a reward and returned to the monitors, switching between feeds and tracking patterns like she had done for the last seven hours.

The answer has to be in here somewhere.

It was five a.m. when she found it.

Three weeks ago, one of the bartenders finished his shift and headed into the service corridor leading to the back of the *Oro Divino* rather leaving out front, like the rest of the staff. An unmarked SUV with tinted windows pulled up at the loading dock entrance in the rear alley a moment later. The bartender opened the bay door and let two men wearing coats with hoods inside the restaurant.

They made for the back stairs, one of the strangers moving with a pronounced limp.

The security cameras on the third floor caught them as they came through a service door. Delphine froze the shot and expanded it. Her eyes narrowed.

The footage from the internal security cameras had a better resolution than the one in the alley. It had captured part of the profile of one of the men.

The guy appeared to be of Caribbean descent.

Delphine pulled up the bartender's file.

His name was Andre Estevez. He was a recent hire and his references looked good on the surface.

A search of the databases of several government agencies showed his real name was Delroy Knight and that he was wanted in connection with several drug trafficking offenses in the US, Mexico, and a string of islands in the Caribbean. His last sighting had been at an airport in Jamaica.

Delphine downloaded the file and frowned at the security camera image. It showed the bartender getting into an unmarked vehicle outside the arrivals lounge. She fed the picture into her mercenary corps database.

Twenty minutes later, she found his destination based on a triangulation from the shots other cameras had caught of the vehicle.

Delphine brought up the address on a satellite map and zoomed in.

It was a luxurious estate with an outdoor pool, a tennis court, a marina, and a helicopter pad. An illegal search of the local utility companies' records showed the property belonged to one Santana Isaacs.

"Got you," she whispered.

Vlad shifted in his sleep beside her, his face peaceful for once. Delphine found herself watching him longer than she should, memorizing the way his lashes fanned against his cheeks and the slight parting of his lips.

She hesitated before reaching out and stroking a gentle finger across his jawline, like she had wanted to do at the restaurant.

Vlad sighed softly and turned into her touch, his breath warming her skin.

Desire and an emotion she refused to identify knotted her belly.

Delphine swallowed hard and got up to make another drink, Tarang's knowing gaze following her.

CHAPTER SEVENTEEN

THE SMELL OF COFFEE AND BACON ROUSED VLAD FROM HIS uncomfortable position on the couch. His neck protested when he lifted his head off the back rest. Papers and laptops littered the coffee table in front of him, evidence of their long night searching through the security footage from the restaurant.

Delphine had cleared the takeout containers and covered him with a blanket.

Vlad blinked groggily and pushed himself up.

Morning light flooded the apartment through the floor-to-ceiling windows. Manhattan was already bustling beyond them.

He checked his watch. It was eight a.m.

Vlad fell back on the couch and closed his eyes. Part of him wanted to believe the last few days had been a dream. That he could pinch himself awake and somehow be in full possession of his powers again. That the curse that had robbed him and Tarang of their magic was nothing but a fading nightmare.

He only had to reach inside himself to confirm that the yawning darkness where his demonic energy should have been was still there.

Tarang's rumble came to him then, along with the quiet sounds of Delphine moving around his kitchen.

"You're worse than my uncle's Rottweiler," the super soldier told the tiger. There was a pause. "No, that wasn't a compliment."

The familiar huffed sheepishly.

The corner of Vlad's mouth lifted despite himself.

It was clear from the last couple of days that Delphine already held a special place in Tarang's heart.

He rose and headed for the kitchen, his steps quiet on the marble floor.

Delphine stood at the stove in fitted black cargo pants and a green sweater that hugged her curves. Her hair was pulled back in the French braid that had first caught his attention at the bar, the tips still wet from a shower. She flipped a pancake with practiced ease.

Tarang sat at her feet with a hopeful expression. His tail started sweeping the floor the instant he spotted Vlad.

"I see you've corrupted my familiar," Vlad drawled.

Delphine glanced over her shoulder, one eyebrow arching in an expression that made awareness prickle his skin.

"He was already corrupt. I caught him trying to steal bacon while my back was turned."

Tarang put on his best innocent face.

"Traitor," Vlad murmured to the tiger. He poured

himself a coffee from the freshly made pot and leaned against the counter. "Did you sleep at all?"

"A little." Delphine transferred the pancake onto a plate already stacked with several others. "I found something interesting in the security footage."

His pulse quickened at her tone. "What kind of something?"

"The kind that explains what happened at the *Oro Divino*." She turned off the stove and faced him, her gaze steady. "Let's eat first."

Vlad helped her carry the food to the island, impatience gnawing at his insides. It wasn't until they'd downed their breakfast that she retrieved her laptop from the lounge and revealed what she'd discovered.

"Your new bartender isn't who he claims to be."

Vlad stiffened. "Andre?"

Delphine's fingers moved quietly on the keyboard. "His real name is Delroy Knight." She turned the screen so he could see. "He's wanted by the DEA for drug trafficking offenses in Mexico, the US, and the Caribbean." Her brow furrowed slightly. "Wanna know something even more interesting? His last location before he showed up in New York and took a job at your place was Kingston, Jamaica."

Heat flushed through Vlad as he stared at the file on the screen, his mind racing at the implication of her words even as he ground his teeth.

Is Wei Chen in on this after all?!

"Show me the security footage," he said in a hard voice.

Delphine pulled it up.

Vlad's knuckles whitened as he watched the bartender

let two men inside the restaurant and guide them to the third floor. Static filled the video when it ended. He met Delphine's calm stare.

"You think that was them casing the joint ahead of the attack?"

"Probably. In which case, one of those men may very well be our sorcerer." She paused, her expression growing strained. "There's something else. I was curious about the video from the night of the attack so I reprocessed it through one of Gideon's servers. We missed a vital clue when we were watching the original recording."

She brought up the footage that had gone viral online and that they'd already seen a dozen times and slowed it right down.

Vlad frowned, not sure what he was seeing at first.

His breath caught when Delphine froze a shot and zoomed in. He leaned forward jerkily.

"Shit. Is that—?!"

Delphine nodded, her eyes tight as she studied the objects that had appeared briefly in the bartender's hands where he stood behind the serving counter in the private dining room. "Delroy had the voodoo dolls on him. My guess is the sorcerer was either in the restaurant or on the service stairs. It's probably why they disabled the interior cameras."

"Were they trying to use Delroy as a scapegoat?" Vlad said between gritted teeth.

"I suspect whoever is behind this whole thing wanted to make sure the sorcerer didn't come to any harm. And having him in the room would have been a dead giveaway. You and Cortes would have sensed he was a sorcerer."

A tense hush fell between them. Delphine broke the silence.

"Someone went to considerable trouble creating Delroy's new identity," she said in a steely voice. "The references he provided check out on paper, but they're all fake. I suspect it was the work of Santana Isaacs, the man he went to visit in Kingston."

The name meant nothing to Vlad.

"I checked the staff roster at the restaurant," Delphine continued with a frown. "Delroy put in a request for leave this week. My guess is he's going to disappear. We need to find him before he leaves the city."

Tarang growled softly beside them, his hackles rising.

Vlad's mouth flattened into a thin line. "I know exactly where to start looking."

CHAPTER EIGHTEEN

"You sure this is the place?" Delphine asked twenty minutes later.

They were parked across from a dingy dive bar in Hell's Kitchen. Though the neon sign above the door was dark, there were signs of movement inside. Steam curled from an extractor fan at the side of the establishment, indicating the kitchen was in use.

"Delroy mentioned this place to Antonio once." Vlad drummed his fingers on the armrest of the Range Rover. "He said it reminded him of home."

Delphine stared. "And you remember that tiny detail because…?"

"Because I make it my business to know everything about the people who work for me." His jaw tightened. "Or I thought I did."

Delphine's phone buzzed. She checked the message on the screen and frowned.

"My contact at the Port Authority confirms Delroy has a flight booked to Kingston tonight."

"Then we better not waste any more time." Vlad reached for the door handle.

Delphine grabbed his wrist, her movement so fast it made him flinch. The contact sent heat dancing across her skin despite the charged situation.

"We do this my way," she said firmly. "You're still vulnerable without your powers."

Vlad scowled. "I can handle myself."

Delphine bit back a curse.

"I don't doubt that." Her grip tightened fractionally. "But we're not taking unnecessary risks. Not this time."

They locked eyes. The air grew thick between them.

Tarang huffed from the back seat, breaking the tension.

"Fine." Vlad relented. "What's the plan?"

"We go in the front. I'll take point." She released his wrist and checked her weapon. "You watch my six and let me do the talking."

"And if he runs?"

A cold smile curved her mouth. "I'd love to see him try."

They exited the vehicle and crossed the road.

The bar's interior reeked of stale beer and cigarettes. A handful of patrons hunched over their drinks at scattered tables, their bleary gazes barely registering their entrance as they watched a baseball game on the TV on the wall. Caribbean music played softly from hidden speakers and the smell of something greasy wafted through the swinging doors leading to the kitchen.

Delphine navigated the floor, her stride purposeful but unhurried.

Vlad and Tarang followed, the familiar invisible to all but the two of them.

The bartender was a heavyset man with tattoos and graying dreadlocks. His eyes narrowed when they approached.

Delphine stopped in front of him, undaunted by his frown.

"We're looking for Andre," she said curtly.

"Don't know no Andre," he grunted.

His voice failed all of her truth detector tells.

"Really? Maybe you know him as Delroy." She placed a mugshot on the counter.

The bartender's expression didn't change.

Had she not been a super soldier, Delphine would have probably missed the infinitesimal flicker in his eyes.

A soft click reached her ears, the sound low enough to be drowned out by the noise from the TV but not so low that it could escape her hearing.

A door marked 'Staff Only' had just closed to the right.

Delphine was already moving.

"Take the back!" she yelled at Vlad.

Vlad unfroze and bolted for the rear exit, Tarang at his heels.

"Hey! You can't go through there!" the bartender roared as Delphine grabbed the handle of the staff door.

It was locked.

She kicked it open, the nanorobots in her peripheral vision catching sight of the bartender as he rounded the counter, a baseball bat in hand and a scowl on his face.

Delphine dashed through the staff area beyond and along a short service corridor that opened into the rear alley.

Delroy was running down the passage to her left.

She went after him.

Vlad burst out of a door ahead of the bartender, Tarang a white shape beside him.

Fear squeezed Delphine's heart when she saw Delroy aim a gun at them.

The army knife strapped to her right ankle appeared in her hand in the blink of an eye.

She never stopped running as she threw it, the metal gleaming dangerously under the sunlight as it left her grip.

Delroy cried out when it impaled the back of his hand a fraction of a second before he pulled the trigger.

The shot went wild.

She was on him in the next moment, anger making her movements harsh as she kicked the back of his leg to bring him to the ground. She slammed his face into the blacktop, breaking his nose. A choked gurgle escaped Delroy when she pinned him with a knee in the small of his back and yanked his arms behind him hard enough to almost dislocate his shoulders.

"Delphine!" Vlad shouted, alarmed.

Air shifted behind her. A draft ruffled her hair and danced across her right cheek as she twisted sharply out of the way of the bartender's down-swinging bat.

Delroy grunted and groaned when it struck his hip.

Delphine rammed his head into the ground when her hand found purchase on his skull. She pushed off fluidly into the air and back-kicked her attacker in the jaw before he could react.

Bone cracked under the heel of her boot.

Delphine somersaulted over Delroy, twisted, and landed lightly on her feet. The bartender struck the ground with his knees and slumped forward.

Vlad appeared beside her.

"Are you okay?!" He grabbed her shoulders, his gaze raking her from head to toe.

"I'm peachy."

Delphine startled when he hugged her tightly to his chest.

"God, that scared me!" Vlad mumbled in her hair.

Delphine stiffened. Every instinct she possessed screamed she should be stepping out of his arms and insisting they keep a professional distance. Yet she found herself standing still, the feel of Vlad's heartbeat pounding against her ribs making her belly clench with an emotion she shouldn't be feeling about a client.

She pulled back and met his worried gaze, remorse tightening her throat.

"Are *you* okay? You almost took a bullet again."

"I'm fine, thanks to you." His eyes glittered. "The way you threw that knife was really hot."

Delphine's breath stuttered as attraction sizzled in the air between them.

Vlad's gaze grew heavy-lidded. He tilted her chin with a knuckle and leaned in to kiss her.

Delphine's lips parted, anticipation sending her pulse racing.

A terrified whimper made them both freeze.

Tarang had sat down on Delroy and was watching them with a grin, heedless of the ashen-faced man frozen beneath him.

A figure appeared at the end of the alley. Delphine tensed before relaxing.

It was Cortes.

"Hey!" the Colombian shouted as he jogged over. "You guys alright?"

Vlad reluctantly released her. "How'd he find us?"

"I messaged him the address."

Popo left Cortes's shoulder and flew ahead of him. He landed on Tarang's head and studied Delroy curiously.

"Who's this punk?" he asked the tiger.

Tarang huffed and growled.

Cortes reached them. "Did I interrupt something?"

His gaze held a hint of curious amusement as it swung between Delphine and Vlad.

"No," she said curtly. She turned and squatted next to Delroy's head. "You really shouldn't have run."

Delroy gulped. "I—I don't know anything!"

Tarang let out a threatening rumble right in his ear.

Delroy yelped. Fear widened his eyes. "Please! They—they'll kill me if I talk!"

Vlad's voice dropped dangerously. "And you think we won't?"

CHAPTER NINETEEN

Delroy huddled in the metal chair, his gaze darting worriedly around the dimly lit cellar.

The *Black Devils* safe house in Brooklyn was a nondescript brownstone housing a laundromat on the ground floor. It looked perfectly normal from the outside. Few people knew the basement contained an interrogation room that could make even the most hardened criminals talk.

Judging from the sheen of sweat on Delroy's face, he'd heard of the place.

"The dolls," Vlad said coldly, straddling the chair opposite the bartender. "Tell us about them."

Delroy swallowed. Blood had crusted around the wound in his hand where Delphine's knife had impaled it. His nose was swollen and deformed, the bruise almost filling the middle of his face.

Vlad would have offered him an ice pack had he not known what a piece of trash the guy was.

"I was given two of them," Delroy confessed, his voice trembling. "Small things, no bigger than my hand. One looked like you." His gaze darted to Tarang. "The other like your tiger."

Vlad's jaw tightened. His familiar's hackles rose where he sat next to him.

"Who gave them to you?" Delphine asked from where she leaned against the wall to the left, her arms crossed.

"I never saw his face." Delroy's shoulders hunched. "He wore a hood every time we met. Walked with a limp." He hesitated. "If I had to guess, I'd say he was middle-aged."

"Is he the same man who came to the restaurant that night three weeks ago?" Vlad said.

Delroy flinched. He licked his lips nervously. "Yes. I heard him chanting something under his breath when he gave me the dolls."

Cortes straightened where he stood near the door. "That guy is definitely our voodoo sorcerer."

Delroy's gaze found Vlad, his expression pleading. "Look, I didn't know what they were planning to do to you! I was just told to keep the dolls on me during my shift. You saw the footage! I almost died during that attack!"

"And yet here you are, alive and well," Vlad snapped.

"'Well' is a matter of opinion," Cortes murmured, glancing at Delphine.

"What happened to the dolls?" Delphine's tone could have frozen hell.

"I— One of the men who attacked the restaurant took them off me before they left." Delroy's panicked gaze flicked to Vlad. "It was the guy who fought you."

Vlad's gut twisted as he recalled the masked man with the saber. Tarang growled.

Delphine lowered her brows. "And the security feeds from the restaurant? The ones that conveniently cut out before they attacked?"

"That wasn't me!" Delroy protested. "Someone else took care of that!"

"Who?" Vlad demanded.

"I don't know!" Terror made Delroy's voice crack. "But that sorcerer guy, he—he works for Santana. That's all I know, I swear!"

Delphine pushed off the wall. "Santana Isaacs?"

Delroy blanched. "You know about him?"

"Only the name." The super soldier crossed the room and rested her hands on the armrests of Delroy's chair. "Tell us about Isaacs."

Delroy leaned back as far as he could, the blood draining from his face.

"Look! I don't know shit about the guy, I swear!" he croaked. "The only thing I can tell you is that he's bad news!"

Delphine studied the squirming man for several tense seconds. She straightened so suddenly Delroy yelped.

"He's telling the truth."

Frustration churned Vlad's insides.

Shit. It's like every inch of progress we make immediately hits a wall!

Time was running out. He now had under thirty-six hours to find the sorcerer who'd cursed him and undo his spell.

The sound of Vlad's cell ringing had Delroy almost jumping out of his chair.

Vlad slipped his phone out of his jacket. He stilled when he saw the number on the screen.

It was Wei Chen.

"We need to talk," the leader of the *Red Dragon* told him curtly when he answered the call.

"Indeed we do." A muscle jumped in his cheek. "I keep hearing your name everywhere these days."

Wei Chen sighed. "It's not what you think it is. I assume you know Jared Dickson?"

"The NYPD Lieutenant?" Vlad's pulse quickened. "What about him?"

"He has a friend who wants to meet with you." Wei Chen paused. "A DEA agent."

Surprise jolted Vlad. His gaze automatically found Delphine.

She was watching him with a focused expression, like she could hear their conversation. She dipped her chin.

"When and where?" Vlad said stiffly.

Wei Chen gave him an address in Lower Manhattan. "One hour."

She hung up.

"What is it?" Cortes asked guardedly.

"Wei Chen wants to meet." Vlad put his phone away, his mind racing. "With us and a DEA agent."

Cortes's pupils flared. "She's working with the DEA?"

Vlad frowned. "It sounds like it."

Cortes's expression turned troubled. "That's not like her at all."

Vlad had to agree. Wei Chen was a proud woman and not one to bow her head to any federal agency. Which meant something had happened that forced her hand into doing so.

"It must be the same agent Jared mentioned," Delphine observed warily. "We should make a move if we want to get there in time for that meeting."

Vlad turned to study Delroy. The bartender had slumped in his chair, relief etched across his face now that Delphine had stepped away from him.

"What do we do with him?" Cortes jerked his head at their prisoner.

"Leave him to my men." Vlad's tone hardened. "They'll make sure he doesn't skip town before the DEA can question him."

Delroy's eyes bulged. "Wait! No! You can't—!"

Vlad was already headed for the door, Tarang at his heels.

"Let's go find out who this Santana Isaacs is."

The address Wei Chen had given them was an upscale dim sum restaurant in Chinatown. Red paper lanterns cast a warm glow over the lacquered furniture and silk screens depicting dragons and phoenixes as Vlad entered the restaurant with Delphine and Cortes.

His scalp prickled.

The place was too quiet, even for a weekday afternoon.

"DEA cleared the place," Delphine murmured as a flustered-looking hostess approached. "There are two agents in the apartment block across the road. Four in the black van outside. Three in the butcher's next door. There are five agents and *Triad* bodyguards in the building with us."

Vlad and Cortes stared.

Cortes arched an eyebrow. "You clocked all that while we were walking here from the car?"

Delphine shrugged. "It's the way I would have set this meeting up."

The hostess led them up the stairs to a private room.

Wei Chen sat at a round table near a window overlooking Mott Street. A man in his forties occupied the chair to her right. Though he wore an expensive suit, his bearing screamed federal agent.

"Vlad." Wei Chen rose, something that looked a little like relief dancing across her face. She indicated the seat opposite her. "Please." She scrutinized Cortes and Delphine. "Him I can understand tagging along. Who's the woman?"

"My new bodyguard," Vlad said curtly.

He settled into the chair she'd indicated, conscious of Delphine taking position slightly behind him. Cortes leaned against the brick wall to the left, Popo watchful on his shoulder.

The DEA guy introduced himself. "Agent Dan Navarro." His shrewd gaze locked on Delphine. "I see Gideon sent his best."

Vlad stiffened. "You know each other?" He glanced warily from Navarro to Delphine.

"Only by reputation." The agent's mouth curved slightly. "Though I suspect that's about to change."

"It's a pleasure to finally meet you," Delphine said with a crisp nod.

The subtle scent of jasmine filled the air as Wei Chen poured tea into delicate porcelain cups. "I believe we all have questions that need answering." She passed him one and gave the other to Navarro.

Vlad picked up the cup and hesitated as he brought it to his lips.

Wei Chen sighed. "It's not poisoned."

"She's right," Delphine murmured. "Besides, she won't make it out of here alive if it is."

Wei Chen's eyes shrank to slits.

"I like her," the Triad leader grunted at Vlad.

Navarro scanned the room warily. "Is your tiger around?"

"He's sitting next to your chair."

Tarang manifested his presence. Wei Chen inhaled sharply.

Vlad had to give it to the DEA agent. Navarro didn't even flinch as he met the tiger's limpid blue stare.

"He's big." Navarro's gaze found Popo. "I've heard stories about the parrot too."

Popo puffed his chest out proudly. Cortes rolled his eyes.

"So, who's going to tell us about Santana Isaacs?" Vlad said coolly, his gaze flicking between Wei Chen and Navarro.

The agent's expression turned inscrutable. "What do you know about him?"

"Only that Wei Chen's Kingston contacts work for him." Vlad's fingers whitened on his cup. "And that he's connected to the man who cursed me."

Wei Chen drew a sharp breath.

Navarro frowned. "That's what made you collapse in that video? A curse?"

"Yes."

Wei Chen recovered her composure. "That's not exactly true. About my Kingston contacts."

CHAPTER TWENTY

"I WAS APPROACHED BY WHAT I THOUGHT WAS A LEGITIMATE business consortium in Kingston six months ago. They wanted to establish trade routes through New York." Wei Chen crossed her legs. "I intended to talk to Yuliy and Giovanni about it if my background investigations proved to be satisfactory."

Delphine watched the Triad leader carefully, looking for any tells that she was lying. She might have trusted Navarro, but she wouldn't bank on Wei Chen being completely truthful in her interactions with them.

So far, the woman appeared to be telling the truth.

"By trade routes, you mean drug routes," Vlad said flatly.

"Yes." Wei Chen's expression hardened. "Whether we like it or not, the Caribbean crime syndicates want in on the East Coast action, Vlad. Better that we supervise their operations than let them run riot around ours."

Vlad lowered his brows.

Delphine broke the strained silence that followed.

"Let me guess. Your background investigations were far from satisfactory."

Wei Chen nodded. "Yes. I discovered the consortium was a front for Santana Isaacs."

Navarro leaned forward. "Isaacs is what we call a ghost crime lord. He's been running one of the most brutal syndicates in the Caribbean for the past fifteen years, but almost no one knows who he is or what he looks like. Those who accidentally do…" He trailed off.

"—end up at the bottom of the ocean," Cortes finished in a chilling voice.

Navarro nodded.

"The man Isaacs hired to act as the leader of his syndicate is a puppet," Wei Chen added. "A very convincing one. If it wasn't for James's instincts, we would have fallen for their ruse."

Vlad scowled. "And you didn't think to mention any of this during our peace negotiations?!"

"I couldn't. I was working with the DEA by then." Wei Chen's face tightened. "My nephew got caught trying to smuggle cocaine through Miami International. Charlie made a mistake, but he's a good kid. This is his first offense. He's the only one in our family who doesn't want to be in the business." She glanced at Navarro. "The DEA offered him a deal on the condition I help set up a sting operation to capture Isaacs."

Vlad clenched his jaw. "You used me as bait."

Navarro ignored his bitter words. "We needed a

legitimate reason for Isaacs to come to New York," he said steadily. "Taking the *Black Devils* down a peg or two was a challenge he couldn't resist, especially considering the benefits he could reap if he were to gain the upper hand."

"Except something went wrong," Delphine said quietly.

The agent's expression grew troubled. "We were planning to capture Isaacs when he attempted something against the *Black Devils*." He hesitated. "We didn't know about the attack or the sorcerer until it was too late."

Delphine's scalp prickled at his tone.

"What aren't you telling us?" Vlad asked stiffly.

Navarro and Wei Chen exchanged a look.

"We just found out that Isaacs's uncle came to New York with him," the agent finally said. "His name is Manuel Isaacs. He disappeared from Haiti fifteen years ago, around the same time Santana started building his empire." His mouth flattened. "Local legend says he practiced magic while in Haiti. The kind that requires a human sacrifice. There are rumors he was behind the disappearance of dozens of women and children who have never been found."

A chill danced down Delphine's spine.

She and the mercenary corps she worked for had dealt with men like Manuel Isaacs plenty of times before. Monsters who deliberately used innocent women and children in their despicable schemes to gain power or maintain it. She'd seen plenty of unmarked graves containing the remains of those who'd lost their lives for a madman's ambitions.

"So Santana Isaacs's rise to power coincided with his

uncle's disappearance from Haiti," she said in a hard voice. "I'm guessing you suspect Manuel's magic played a part in that."

"We believe so." Navarro's expression grew grim. "Every rival who stood in Santana's way died under mysterious circumstances. Some went mad. A few wasted away from unknown diseases. Others simply vanished."

"Like those women and children in Haiti," Cortes said darkly.

Delphine noted Vlad's white knuckles underneath the table. She clamped down on the urge to touch his shoulder and focused on the conversation.

"You have to believe me, Vlad." Wei Chen's face tightened. "I didn't know about Isaacs's uncle until yesterday."

A muscle jumped in Vlad's cheek.

"We've been trying to get to Santana Isaacs for years," Navarro said, a hint of an apology in his voice. "This was our best shot."

"Your best shot went sideways in a major way," Vlad grated out. "And now I have less than thirty-six hours to break this damn curse before it becomes permanent!"

Wei Chen paled. "The curse can become permanent?"

"Yes," Vlad said bitterly.

Navarro grimaced guiltily. "The reason we called you over is because we found out where Isaacs might be hiding and we'd like you guys to assist us in taking him and his men down." The agent removed a file from his jacket and placed it on the table. "We've been monitoring a property in Queens. Our surveillance suggests Isaacs is using it as his base of operations in New York. Rumor on the grapevine is they have a boat coming to pick them up soon." He opened the folder and pushed it toward Vlad.

Delphine's pulse quickened as she studied the photographs it contained.

The building was a three-story warehouse near the waterfront.

"How sure are you about this intel?" she asked the agent sharply.

"Very." Navarro indicated one of the images. "That guy is rumored to be Santana's right-hand man. And those"—he pointed at three figures in dark clothes entering through a side door—"are his enforcers."

"When was this taken?" Vlad demanded.

"Yesterday morning." Navarro's expression hardened. "We believe Santana himself arrived in New York five days ago."

The hairs lifted on the back of Delphine's neck. She exchanged a startled look with Vlad and Cortes.

That would coincide with the attack at the *Oro Divino*.

Vlad's next words sent a jolt of surprise through her.

"Give us twenty-four hours," the incubus told Navarro in a steely voice. "Let us deal with this our way first."

The agent frowned. "This operation is ours to lead in the first place. There's no way we're letting you guys go in there on your own."

"Vlad is right," Delphine said with a frown. "Considering they managed to give you guys the slip and attacked the *Oro Divino*, it could be there's a mole in your agency."

"She has a point," Wei Chen murmured in the tense hush.

The lines around Navarro's eyes tightened.

"I can't deny that possibility," the agent admitted grudgingly.

"They'll be looking out for a large sting operation," Delphine said. "We'll have a better chance eliminating them with a small group of people."

"And a tiger," Wei Chen murmured.

Navarro drummed his fingers on the table.

"Look, you have nothing to lose," Cortes said with a shrug. "You can be the backup if you're that worried about us."

Navarro made a face. "The only time you'll ever need backup is if Hell freezes over."

Cortes smiled flintily.

Navarro deflated, his expression suggesting he was acting against his best judgment. "You have eighteen hours. After that, we move in." He pushed back his chair and rose. "I'll be in touch. Good luck."

They watched the agent leave.

"Is he always that blunt?" Vlad said to no one in particular.

"Yes." Wei Chen sighed at Vlad's cool stare. "I truly am sorry about what happened."

"Save it," Vlad snapped. "I thought we were friends." He narrowed his eyes. "You used me."

"Yes, I did." The Triad leader met his gaze without flinching. "And I'll pay you back for it."

"There is only one way you can pay me back," Vlad grunted.

Wei Chen steeled herself. "What do you want?"

"We're finishing that peace talk when this is all over."

Wei Chen blinked at the incubus's gruff words. Her shoulders relaxed. She smiled faintly. "Alright." Her smile faded a little. "But Marco stays home this time." She shuddered. "I hate that little toad."

CHAPTER TWENTY-ONE

Delphine studied the warehouse two hundred feet away through her night-vision goggles. The heat signatures of the men patrolling the perimeter of the property brightened the 3D display, the nanorobots in her retina enhancing the signal further.

"I count fifteen outside," she murmured. "Twelve more inside the building."

"That's a lot of muscle for a warehouse that's supposed to be empty," Cortes said quietly beside her. "Looks like Navarro was right on the money."

The two of them were crouched in the shadows of a loading dock across the street, the twelve-man-strong *Black Devils* team spread out in strategic positions around them. Vlad and Tarang were next to an adjacent building.

All of the men were equipped with the nanorobot vests and the enhanced night-vision goggles her mercenary corps used in combat situations. As for Delphine, she wore her bespoke liquid armor suit, the dark material absorbing the ambient moonlight where it clung to her body.

Cortes's phone vibrated. He checked the screen and frowned.

"It's Bryony."

Vlad's tense voice came through Delphine's earpiece. "Connect her via speaker."

Delphine switched Cortes's call to their comm network.

"Is Vlad with you?" Bryony said sharply when Cortes answered. "I can't reach him."

"I'm here," Vlad said over the connection. "We're about to storm the place where the sorcerer is hiding."

Bryony sighed, her relief evident. "Good! Because we just discovered two pieces of crucial information about that curse."

Tension knotted Delphine's shoulders.

"What is it?" Vlad asked stiffly.

"The dolls need to be destroyed by fire. And you have to be the one to do it."

A strained hush followed.

"That could be a problem," Vlad said curtly. "I'm not exactly in possession of my powers right now."

"No, you don't understand." Urgency underscored Bryony's voice. "You need to *burn* the dolls. With regular fire. The act of destruction has to come from you specifically for the curse to be fully undone."

Delphine's pulse quickened. She met Cortes's gaze.

"So, we need to get the dolls to Vlad?" the Colombian stated in a hard voice.

"Yes." Bryony hesitated. "And you have to hurry. Mrs.

Son-Ha got the countdown wrong. The window for breaking the curse is closing faster than she'd estimated."

Vlad cursed softly in Russian.

Dread churned Delphine's stomach. "How much time do we have?"

"Four hours. Maybe less." Bryony paused. "My best guess is sunrise."

Delphine checked her watch. Two-seventeen a.m. Adrenaline surged through her veins, focusing her mind. "Understood. Anything else?"

"No." Bryony hesitated. "Good luck." She ended the call.

Delphine touched her earpiece. "Change of plans. I'm going after the sorcerer and the dolls alone. The rest of you focus on Isaacs and his men."

"Like hell you are!" Vlad snapped across the comm.

Cortes frowned at her. "That's a bad idea." Popo ruffled his feathers uneasily on his shoulder.

"It makes more sense tactically," she said firmly. "I can move faster on my own." She transmitted the thermal imaging overlaying her goggles to them and their team. "Those heat signatures are concentrated in two locations: the office block on the east side of the building and what looks like a converted storage area on the west side."

Cortes's mouth pressed to a thin line. "The sorcerer will be in the storage area. It's more isolated."

"I agree. Which means Isaacs is in the office block." She met the Colombian's gaze. "Between you and Vlad, you should go after him. The guy might have some magic tricks up his sleeve." Delphine switched channels on their comm. "Team Two, what's your status?"

"In position," one of the *Black Devils* replied. "We have eyes on the loading bay on the water."

"Team Three?"

"North entrance is covered," another voice confirmed.

She touched her earpiece again, her voice steady. "Vlad? It's your call."

There was a short silence.

"Is this our best strategy?" Vlad ground out.

"Yes."

"I don't like it." A frustrated sigh came down the line. "But we'll do as you say." The incubus paused. "Del?"

"Yeah?"

"Be careful."

Heat pooled in her belly at the concern in his voice.

"You too." She drew her weapon, checked the magazine, and glanced at Cortes. "On five."

They rose on her countdown and dashed off in opposite directions.

Delphine moved like a ghost to the edge of the property, the layout of the area and the patrolling guards clear through the crisp view of her goggles. She waited until two men passed before silently scaling the fence and slipping behind a stack of shipping containers.

The warehouse loomed ahead, its dark bulk casting deep shadows across the yard. She picked up the sound of waves lapping at the wharf beyond the building.

There was movement on her left.

Delphine dropped and pressed her back against the metal wall of a container as another patrol rounded the corner. The men were oblivious to her presence as they walked past her hiding spot, their low voices carrying clearly in the breeze coming off the water.

"—said the boss wants us ready to move at dawn."

"Yeah, well, I ain't looking forward to that boat ride back to Kingston."

Delphine frowned. Navarro had been right.

Isaacs was leaving in the morning.

The guards disappeared at the far end of the container stack.

She rounded the container, tapped her goggles, and adjusted the 3D perspective of the floor plan and thermal imaging she was picking up through the warehouse walls. The storage area where she suspected Manuel was hiding showed five heat signatures. Four were moving in patrol patterns. The fifth remained stationary in what appeared to be the center of the space.

That has to be him.

Delphine scanned the yard before closing the distance to the warehouse in a low crouch. She reached the side of the building and found what she was looking for—a maintenance access ladder leading to the roof.

She was mapping the quickest route to her target through the warehouse's ventilation system when gunfire erupted from the front of the building.

"Contact!" Cortes barked over the comm. "East side!"

More shots rang out, from the north this time. Shouts of alarm followed as Isaacs's men clocked that there were intruders on the premises.

Delphine scaled the ladder swiftly as chaos erupted below. The distraction would give her the window she needed to get to Manuel.

Let's just hope he stays put and doesn't bolt.

She reached the roof without being spotted and headed for the ventilation duct. The access panel was screwed on tight. She ripped it out with sheer brute force, her enhanced strength making short work of the bolts securing it.

Delphine slipped down into a tunnel and had crawled some fifty feet when her scalp prickled. She stilled, her nanorobots picking up on something just beyond the limit of their perception. Something strange.

"It's that damn magic again!" Cortes barked on the comm amid the sound of gunfire. "That sorcerer must be up to something!"

"Delphine?" Vlad asked urgently.

She clenched her jaw and accelerated, her pulse racing. "I'm on it."

She took a couple of turns, slid down a duct, and reached the high-ceilinged storage area she'd been aiming for.

The ventilation shaft opened in the northwest corner of the room.

Delphine peered through the grating.

The space had been cleared except for a circle of candles on the concrete floor. Manuel Isaacs stood within it, his hands raised as he chanted in a language she didn't recognize, the flickering light casting eldritch shadows across his weathered face. Four armed men were spaced out amidst the boxes and crates piled haphazardly around the room, weapons at the ready as they protected the sorcerer.

Delphine stilled when she spotted an object tucked in

Manuel's belt. It was a small pouch. One that could easily hold two voodoo dolls.

She loosened the grating silently, her eyes on the guards. Their attention was focused toward the door and the sounds of fighting echoing throughout the building.

Delphine dropped nimbly from the ventilation shaft and rolled across the floor into the cover of a stack of crates. She rose, her movements fluid, a shadow in the night.

The first guard never knew what hit him.

She caught him as he fell and eased his body to the ground, his neck crooked in death.

One down.

The second man turned just as she reached him. Delphine's knife found his throat before he could raise the alarm, the blade carving through his jugular and his windpipe in a slick motion.

Two.

The remaining guards spotted her when she emerged from the shadows. They opened fire.

Delphine was already moving. She dove, rolled beneath the spray of bullets, and came up inside the nearest man's guard. Her elbow caught him in the solar plexus and her hand found his weapon as he doubled over.

A bullet smashed into her nanorobot suit as her finger slipped smoothly inside the trigger. The shot crumpled on contact, raising a curse from the man who'd fired at her. She shifted smoothly behind the guard she'd struck in the chest and used his body as a shield just as the fourth man fired again. The guard jerked in her hold as shots peppered him.

She took out the fourth man with a shot to the head.

He fell, dead before he hit the ground.

Three and four.

Manuel's chanting grew frantic as she stepped into the open area where he stood, his eyes dark with fear and loathing. He flung out a hand toward her.

Nothing happened.

The sorcerer's eyes widened when she kept advancing.

"Yeah, that won't work on me," Delphine said coldly.

She ripped her night-vision goggles from her face and crossed the circle of candles in three long strides. Manuel backpedaled, his limp pronounced as he tried to escape.

Delphine's fist caught him in the jaw. The sorcerer grunted and collapsed to the floor.

She snatched the pouch from his belt and emptied it.

Fury brought a burn of bile to her throat when two crude cloth dolls fell into her palm, one human-shaped, the other a tiger. She clenched her jaw at the sight of the blood marks staining them and the hair poking through the material.

Something jumped on Delphine's leg and attempted to bite her.

Teeth cracked as the liquid armor suit blocked the attempt. Manuel's familiar revealed its presence, the weasel's eyes full of fear and rage.

Delphine grabbed it and stuffed it inside the pouch.

"I've got the dolls," she said tersely into her comm.

Static crackled in response.

She frowned and tried again. "Vlad? Cortes?!"

White noise filled her earpiece.

The sounds of fighting had grown closer. Delphine slipped her goggles back on and zeroed in on the heat signatures in the warehouse.

They were concentrated in the east block, where Isaacs should be, and in the center of the building.

Tension knotted her shoulders. She needed to get the dolls to Vlad.

A groan made her turn. Manuel was pushing himself to his knees, blood trickling from his split lip.

"You have no idea what you're dealing with!" he spat.

"Actually, I do." Delphine took a zip-tie from her utility belt, secured the sorcerer's hands behind his back, and gagged him before hauling him to his feet. "Let's go find your nephew."

She'd just stepped out of the storage room with Manuel when a distant detonation shook the building. Her pulse spiked.

Vlad!

CHAPTER TWENTY-TWO

Vlad swooped beneath a knife, slammed his shoulder into his attacker's chest, and sent the man flying into a wall. He raised his gun and shot him point-blank in the chest. The man slumped to the ground.

Sweat stung his eyes as he and the *Black Devils* fought their way through the warehouse, his muscles burning from exertion and his breaths coming hard and fast. Tarang was a white blur beside him, the tiger's fangs and claws finding flesh and bone as he took down anyone who stood in their path.

It felt wrong fighting without their powers. Even through their muted bond, Vlad could tell Tarang was experiencing the same frustrating feeling.

It was like trying to breathe with only one lung.

Gunfire erupted up ahead. Vlad dove behind a stack of crates with his men. Tarang darted inside the gap between two containers.

Vlad cursed as bullets pinged off metal and concrete around them.

One caught a *Black Devils* guard in the flank. The man grunted as the shot crumpled and slid to the ground. Even though the nanorobot vests protected their vital organs, they did not completely shield them from the impact of any bullets they took.

Vlad signaled to his men. They shifted position around the crates and returned fire, forcing the figures shooting at them to take cover. It was all the time Tarang needed to leap from the boxes he'd silently scaled.

Vlad reloaded his gun while the enemies' terrified screams rent the air.

"Status?!" he barked into his comm.

"North block secured," one of his men replied tersely. "Moving to support Team Two."

"We've got eyes on Isaacs!" Cortes's voice crackled in Vlad's earpiece. "Second floor office. He's—*shit!*"

Popo squawked in the background.

The connection cut out at the same time a detonation shook the building.

Vlad's stomach dropped, his gaze swiveling in the direction of the east block. "Cortes?!"

The only answer he got was a bunch of static. Movement to his left had him twisting sharply and bringing his gun up. He relaxed fractionally when he recognized three of his men.

"The Colombian needs backup," he told them urgently. "Get to the east block. Take a team with you."

They nodded and moved out.

Vlad scanned the warehouse, his jaw tight. Something

was interfering with their comms. More worryingly, he hadn't heard from Delphine in over ten minutes.

Tarang made a soft sound as he returned to his side and bumped his leg. Vlad touched the tiger's head briefly.

"I know. Let's go find her." He turned to the *Black Devils* men with him. "Keep them occupied. I'm going to check out the west block."

The guards exchanged wary glances.

"I don't think that's such a good idea, boss," one of them said. "We promised Ilya and Milo nothing would happen to you."

"I'll be fine. Tarang's with me."

Vlad didn't wait for their answer.

They watched uneasily as he and Tarang melted into the shadows.

The sound of gunfire faded as Vlad crossed the warehouse toward the location of the storage area, Tarang a silent shape by his side. They'd just passed the halfway point when movement ahead made him freeze.

The hairs lifted on the back of his neck.

Tarang stopped and growled.

A masked figure emerged from the gloom, moonlight gleaming off the weapon in his hand.

Vlad's pulse quickened. It was a saber. One he recognized.

"Well, well." The man's amused voice carried across the space between them, his accent telling. "If it isn't the *Black Devils'* powerless heir."

Vlad's fingers whitened on his gun. The suspicion he'd had since meeting Navarro solidified into certainty.

"Santana Isaacs, I presume?"

The man ignored his deadly tone, his stance relaxed as he approached. "I'm surprised you made the connection so fast." He reached up and removed his mask.

Vlad's stomach churned with rage when he finally saw the face of the man who'd had him cursed.

"What did you do to Cortes?!"

Santana smirked. "Oh, your sorcerer friend? I buried him and your men under a pile of rubble. Pretty sure I killed his annoying parrot too."

Air shifted beside Vlad. Tarang leapt with a furious roar.

Alarm choked his breath. *"No!"*

He reached for the tiger, his fingers closing on empty space.

Santana crushed an object in his hand.

Tarang dropped mid-leap, a grunt of pain leaving him. His body landed on the concrete floor with a sickening thud.

Vlad rushed over to his familiar, his heart slamming against his ribs. He dropped to his knees and touched the tiger's neck with a trembling hand.

Relief made him weak.

Tarang's pulse thrummed rapidly beneath his fingers. The tiger opened an eye and gave him a glazed look, his rib cage moving with a shuddering motion.

Rage replaced fear. Vlad twisted around and glared at Santana.

"What the hell did you do to him, asshole?!"

Santana moved with a speed that belied his lithe frame. Vlad barely managed to dodge the saber as it whistled past his face. He stumbled back, raised his gun, and fired.

The crime lord twisted in a motion that should not have been humanly possible, avoiding the shots. His blade found Vlad's weapon and sent it flying, the edge slicing a deep cut in Vlad's palm.

"You're not the only one with special abilities." Santana's eyes shone with an unholy light as he circled him. "My uncle's magic has granted me a few tricks of my own." He lunged.

Vlad covered Tarang with his body and blocked the next strike with his back. The nanorobot vest absorbed most of the impact. His heel found Santana's shin. The crime lord cursed and fell back.

Tarang's labored breathing filled Vlad's ears, each one weaker than the last. Fear clawed at his insides. He could feel their muted connection growing fainter.

He climbed to his feet and turned to face Santana.

"Tell me what you did to him!" Vlad snarled.

Santana's smile was pure evil. "The same thing I'm about to do to you."

He reached inside his pocket and removed a second object.

Vlad's stomach plummeted when he finally discerned their shapes.

They were crude voodoo dolls, no bigger than his thumb. The one Santana had crushed resembled a tiger. The other was human-shaped.

"My uncle made these for me." Santana held up the tiger doll. "An insurance policy, in case the ones we had Delroy carry failed." His fingers tightened on it. "I must say, watching your familiar suffer is quite entertaining."

Tarang whimpered.

Fury and terror churned Vlad's gut. He charged Santana with a roar.

The crime lord danced out of reach, his laughter ringing mockingly in Vlad's ears as he avoided his strikes with unnatural grace.

"You're good. But not good enough without your powers!"

His fist found Vlad's jaw. Stars exploded across Vlad's vision. He hit the ground hard and rolled on instinct, avoiding the saber by a hairbreadth as it stabbed into the concrete where his head had been.

"I was going to let the curse do its work." A mad gleam brightened Santana's gaze. "But killing you might serve my purpose better!"

He crushed the human-shaped doll's chest.

Agony exploded inside Vlad's body. He screamed, his back arching off the floor, white-hot pain squeezing his ribcage and causing black dots to swarm his vision. He gasped for air in vain, his lungs refusing to work.

Santana's face appeared above him, the crime lord's expression distorted in a savage grin.

"I hear Hell is nice this time of year," he said gleefully.

The saber rose, moonlight dancing along its deadly edge as it descended toward Vlad's neck.

A knife flashed through the air and impaled Santana's hand.

Santana cursed and jerked away, blood spraying from the wound. His weapon clattered to the floor. The dolls fell from his grip as he clutched his bleeding limb and whirled around.

"How about you get away from him?" Delphine's voice was pure steel as she stepped into a patch of moonlight.

❄

Delphine slipped a second blade from the sheath on her thigh while Santana hastily retrieved his saber. Her gaze darted to Vlad where he'd rolled onto his front and was hugging the ground. The incubus raised his head, his face ashen.

"Glad to see you're okay," he mumbled with a weak smile.

"You look terrible."

Vlad laughed. "I've been better." A violent coughing fit racked his body and made him groan.

Delphine clocked the bloodied, miniature voodoo dolls next to the incubus and glanced at Tarang's shuddering form. An emotion she rarely felt and always managed to control swept through her like a storm then, breaking the dam of her iron self-control.

For once, she did not fight it.

Heat flushed through her, her fury focusing her every sense.

Santana's face contorted with rage at the sight of his injured uncle lying on the ground behind Delphine.

"You'll pay for that!" the crime lord snarled.

His blade flashed as he charged her, his speed and agility boosted by whatever magic his sorcerer uncle had weaved.

Delphine tracked the trajectory of his strike before he'd completed the motion. She twisted smoothly out of the way and danced lightly past his guard. The heel of her palm found his solar plexus at the same time she slashed a cut across his left temple.

Santana grunted and stumbled, blood streaming freely down the side of his face.

Delphine swooped in to attack. The saber sang past her skull.

She leaned back sharply, the edge missing her head by millimeters.

Delphine narrowed her eyes. "So, your uncle's magic doesn't just improve your fighting skills. It increases your pain threshold."

Santana bared his teeth and came at her with a furious sound. His next attack took the form of a flurry of strikes that would have overwhelmed a normal opponent.

It was no match for the Immortal DNA and nanorobots flowing through her veins.

Delphine blocked and parried with her knife, her movements fluid and precise as she matched him blow for blow.

Fury and confusion warred in Santana's eyes as he failed to land a single blow. He retreated a couple of steps and licked his lips.

"Who the hell are you?!"

A savage half-smile curved Delphine's mouth. "Me?" She jerked her head toward Vlad. "I'm just his bodyguard."

She feinted left, ducked under Santana's guard, and rammed her knee into his gut. The crime lord doubled over with a wheeze. Her uppercut caught him in the jaw and sent him staggering back.

Delphine's hand found her utility belt. She grabbed the

dolls she'd taken from Manuel and the lighter she always carried.

"Vlad! Catch!" she barked as she tossed them over.

The incubus looked up where he was slowly rising from the ground. His pupils flared.

Santana's eyes widened. "No!"

He lunged for the items.

Her roundhouse kick caught him in the chest and sent him flying.

Vlad's trembling fingers closed around the dolls and the lighter. He reached for the bloodied miniature dolls.

Santana climbed back to his feet and charged at the incubus with an enraged scream, his saber a silver arc as it carved the air.

Delphine blocked his attack.

The click of the lighter when it came sounded unnaturally loud in the gloom of the warehouse.

The scent of burning cloth and hair filled her nostrils.

Santana screamed.

The ground trembled as a violent force detonated across the warehouse, its power warming her flesh on a crimson haze.

CHAPTER TWENTY-THREE

Heat exploded inside Vlad's body as the dolls burned brightly and turned to ash on the ground before him. The tidal wave of energy that surged through his veins from his reawakened core made him gasp and arch. His blood sang and his heart soared as his incubus magic roared back to life, filling the void that had left him feeling hollow these past days.

The bond he'd shared with Tarang since they were small flared like a supernova. The tiger stirred and rose, shaking himself off as if waking from a long sleep.

The triumphant roar that left his familiar brought dust down from the rafters. Tarang's eyes blazed crimson, demonic energy crackling across his white fur.

Vlad's pulse raced with elation as their cores connected, the power that was theirs and theirs alone to wield the sweetest thing he'd ever tasted. His gaze found Santana as he rose, his brief moment of joy replaced by a fury that made the very air around him shimmer.

"You tried to kill my familiar." His voice dropped dangerously as he faced the crime lord. "You tried to kill *me*. And you almost succeeded."

Delphine pulled back to give them space, a small smile playing on her lips as she watched him.

Vlad's heart clenched at the look in her eyes. The super soldier's steady gaze was full of confidence that he would see this through and something else that made a different kind of fire lick through his veins.

There was motion opposite him.

Santana backpedaled across the ground, his face draining of color as he registered the red aura surrounding Vlad. His gaze darted to Manuel's unconscious form.

"Uncle!" Fear cracked his voice. "Manuel! *Wake up!*"

"He can't help you now." One of the diamond studs in Vlad's ears transformed at his silent command, the gleaming sword humming with deadly intent as it dropped eagerly into his hand. "No one can."

Santana grasped his saber with trembling fingers and pushed up to his feet.

"Stay back! *Stay away from me, you monster!*" he shrieked.

Vlad narrowed his eyes. "You think I'm the monster? Then allow me to demonstrate exactly what this monster can do."

Tarang's pupils blazed with unholy fire as he lent Vlad his strength.

Vlad moved.

Santana barely managed to block his first strike. The second shattered his saber into a dozen pieces. The crime lord tripped and stumbled, terror overwhelming whatever magical ability his uncle had granted him.

Tarang's snarl filled the air as he circled behind their enemy.

"Please!" Santana dropped to his knees, his body quaking. "I'll give you anything you want! Money! Power!" He gazed pleadingly at Vlad.

"I already have both," Vlad growled. "What I want is revenge."

Santana screamed as demonic magic detonated around him, the crimson tide lifting him off his feet and slamming him into a stack of crates. Wood splintered. The crime lord slumped to the ground with a groan.

"Get up." Vlad stalked toward him, his blade trailing scarlet static on the concrete floor. "I'm not done with you yet."

Santana staggered to his feet and tried to run.

Tarang cut off his escape. Santana whirled around wildly, only to find Vlad right behind him.

"You know what the worst part is?" Vlad gritted his teeth. "You made me feel helpless."

His fist caught Santana in the jaw. The crime lord flew across the floor and struck a support beam with a sickening crunch. Blood sprayed from his lips.

"You made me doubt myself."

Vlad's next punch drove the air from Santana's lungs.

"And, of all the stupid things you could have done"—he grabbed the crime lord by the throat and lifted him off his feet—"you hurt my friends."

Santana clawed weakly at Vlad's fingers, his face turning purple.

Tarang issued a warning growl that made the incubus pause.

Delphine frowned at the shadows in the west end of the warehouse.

"DEA's here."

Figures in tactical vests emerged from the gloom, weapons trained on them. Navarro was in the lead. The agent slowed and lowered his gun when he saw them, his face relaxing slightly.

Vlad frowned. "You said you'd give us eighteen hours."

"I lied," Navarro said, unabashed.

"More like he was worried about us," someone said. "If the *Black Devils* heir died on his watch, there'd be hell to pay."

Vlad's head snapped around.

Cortes was limping toward them. He was covered in dust and sported a cut above his eye. Popo looked similarly disheveled on his shoulder.

Relief lightened Vlad's chest. "I thought you were dead."

"Almost was." Cortes grimaced. "That explosion buried us under half a wall. If it wasn't for Popo manifesting a shield at the last second—"

"My Enrique would have been squished like a bug!" the parrot declared proudly.

This earned the bird wary looks from several DEA agents.

Navarro jerked his head. "How about you let him go before you kill him?"

Vlad turned. Santana's eyes had rolled back in his head.

He curled his lip and dropped the crime lord.

Santana crumpled to the ground with a wheeze.

Navarro cuffed him and read him his rights while another agent arrested Manuel.

"Boss," someone called out.

Vlad turned. One of the *Black Devils* was jogging toward them, the rest following in his wake.

"What's our men's status?" the incubus asked tensely.

"Some broken bones, a few scratches and bruises." The guy shrugged. "Nothing that won't heal."

Vlad breathed a sigh of relief.

The DEA agents eyed the nanorobot vests the *Black Devils* were wearing with envious looks.

"Those must have cost an arm and a leg," Navarro muttered.

"I called in a personal favor with Gideon," Delphine said dismissively.

The DEA agent made a face. "How come he doesn't do those for the US government?"

"Because you guys can afford to be bled dry," the super soldier said succinctly.

"Ouch." Navarro eyed the tiger circling the warehouse before glancing guardedly at the dark sword in Vlad's hand. "So does this mean you have your powers back?"

"I do. And I have you to thank for that, even though you were actually responsible for me losing them in the first place."

Navarro sighed. "You're never gonna let that go, are you?"

Vlad arched an eyebrow. "And lose the chance for the DEA to owe me a favor?"

One of the *Black Devils* approached, his cell in hand and his expression mystified. "Hey, boss? There's a crazy lady on the phone asking if you got your juju back yet."

The sound of enthusiastic yipping issued from the speaker.

"That's gotta be Mrs. Son-Ha," Cortes muttered.

Vlad took his cell out of his back pocket. It was smashed to pieces.

He frowned. "How did she even get that number?"

Another guy put his hand up warily and showed them his phone. "Er, boss? Someone claiming to be the head of a coven is saying you've got ninety minutes to sunrise, so how about you get your ass into gear and break that curse pronto."

Cortes snorted. Vlad muttered something under his breath.

"Your friends are charming," Navarro remarked.

Delphine's phone buzzed. She checked the screen. "It's Yuliy."

CHAPTER TWENTY-FOUR

THE SUN WAS RISING OVER BROOKLYN WHEN THEY DROVE onto the grounds of the mansion.

Gustav and Lena were at the front door, their expressions anxious. Relief brightened their eyes at the sight of Vlad and Tarang emerging from an SUV.

Yuliy was waiting in the foyer, tension evident in the tight lines framing his eyes. The *Black Devils'* boss crossed the floor and squeezed his nephew to his chest wordlessly.

Vlad shuddered and hugged his uncle just as tightly.

"I'm back," he whispered.

Delphine knew he meant the words in more than one sense.

Tarang rumbled and pressed affectionately against Yuliy's leg.

The older man's shoulders loosened. He released Vlad and stroked the tiger's head, his face softening.

Yuliy met Delphine's gaze. "Thanks for keeping them safe."

She dipped her head curtly. "Just doing my job."

She'd changed into her business suit, her hair tied back in a slick ponytail.

Delphine caught the look Vlad shot her way and refused to acknowledge it. Her mission was over and she was going back to Washington.

That prospect should have pleased her.

Yet the only thing she was feeling was a hollowness that was growing deeper with every passing hour. She knew damn well the cause of it was the man watching her with a guarded expression.

Lena served breakfast in the dining room overlooking the marina while Vlad gave his uncle a debrief about the night's events.

Though Yuliy had been furious about the DEA operation and Wei Chen's involvement in it when they'd spoken with him before putting together a team to go after Santana, he'd agreed that having the Triad leader and the federal agency in their debt would serve them well in the long run.

They broached the topic of the peace negotiations between Wei Chen and the Lucianos presently.

"Maybe I should ask Miss Dubois to stick around for the next meeting," Yuliy suggested. His shrewd gaze swung between Delphine and Vlad.

Lena paused expectantly, coffeepot half tilted toward the *Black Devils*' leader's cup. The piece of bacon poised on the tip of Gustav's fork hovered near his mouth as he stared.

"You will have to discuss that with Gideon," Delphine

said in a level voice. "Besides, I believe Ilya and Milo will be back in action by then, so you won't be in need of my services." She focused on her plate, conscious of Vlad's frown.

"Does that mean you're leaving New York?" the incubus asked stiffly.

"Yes."

His frown deepened. "When?"

"It depends."

He crushed the napkin in his hand. "On what?" he fairly growled.

Yuliy, Gustav, and Lena watched with bated breath, their gazes swinging across the table. So did Tarang's.

Heat crawled up Delphine's neck. She narrowed her eyes at Vlad.

"I don't owe you an answer."

Her cool tone made his jaw tighten. "I see."

Vlad pushed back his chair and strode out of the room, his spine rigid. Tarang hesitated before leaving his plate of steak and padding after him. A nervous huff left the tiger as he glanced at Delphine over his shoulder.

Delphine closed her eyes briefly.

This is why I don't do relationships. They complicate everything.

Yet the thought of walking away from what she and Vlad had started made her chest ache in a way she'd never experienced before. She hated to admit it, but she cared for the incubus.

And the tiger. And even the Black Devils.

"Dammit," she muttered.

Her fork groaned as it bent in her grip.

Yuliy looked fairly impressed at the feat.

"You made a terrible mess of that," Lena told Delphine bluntly.

Yuliy looked up from the twisted cutlery. "To be fair, Vlad's equally at fault. He was never good at talking about his feelings."

"Remember that time he had that crush on that little girl in kindergarten?" Gustav mused.

Lena grimaced. "You mean when he put a toad in her bag and mud in her lunch box and then was upset when she told the teacher and got him in trouble?"

A reminiscent smile curved Yuliy's mouth. "He cried for a whole day after he got his heart broken." He chuckled. "He was a cute little devil."

Delphine's mouth pressed to a thin line. "You guys are not helping."

The drive back to Vlad's apartment was a tense affair.

Delphine glanced at the incubus where he sat in the passenger seat, his cold profile gilded by the morning light. Tarang was curled up asleep in the back, having evidently decided that matters of the human heart were far too exhausting to contemplate on a full stomach.

She broke the silence first.

"Look, I apologize. I shouldn't have said what I said back there."

"Which part?" His pupils flashed crimson as he looked at her.

Now that his powers had fully returned, she could feel a subtle heat emanating from him. One that made her skin tingle and her pulse quicken.

Serena had told her super soldiers were immune to magic, including Vlad's incubus charm. Which meant what she was feeling was one hundred percent her own emotion.

Her fingers tightened on the steering wheel of the Range Rover.

Delphine Dubois, you need to grow a pair.

She took a deep breath. "I like you."

The confession made Vlad freeze. He blinked, like he couldn't believe what she'd just said.

"What?" he breathed.

"I said I like you," she ground out.

He hesitated. "You mean, like…a friend?"

Delphine scowled. "Friends do not do what I did to you three nights ago. Four times."

Color stained Vlad's cheekbones. His expression turned serious. "I like you too."

Delphine's heart clenched. "You mean that?"

"Pull over."

She blinked. "What?"

"Pull over, Delphine." His eyes flared scarlet, his tone dropping to an octave that made her shiver.

Delphine swallowed, checked the mirrors, and pulled into a service lane.

She'd barely engaged the handbrake when Vlad undid his seat belt, leaned over the center console, and clasped her face.

He claimed her mouth in a kiss that made her blood sing. She melted against him with a soft sound, her hands rising to sink into his hair.

It was a while before they came up for air.

They stared at one another, desire setting the space between them alight.

"How fast can you get us to the apartment?" Vlad mumbled, his face flushed and his pupils liquid fire.

Delphine steered her thoughts in the right direction with some difficulty and did a quick mental calculation.

"Twenty minutes."

Vlad nipped at her lip with his teeth, making her belly clench all over again. "I know a shortcut."

They made it there in fifteen and barely managed to get inside the elevator before they were all over each other again, their mouths hungry and their touch desperate. Tarang padded straight to a sunny spot on the upstairs landing the moment they entered the apartment, evidently intent on giving them their privacy this time.

Delphine pushed Vlad against the wall like she'd done the first night and began popping the buttons of his shirt. She made an impatient sound when she got halfway down and ripped the whole thing off his chest.

Vlad chuckled as buttons went flying everywhere.

"You know, that's a very expensive Armani shirt."

"Bill me." Delphine kicked her boots off while he stripped her shirt off her shoulders, his eyes bright with desire as he stared at the lace covering her bare skin.

Her hands found his belt buckle.

Vlad's breathing accelerated, his gaze growing heavy-lidded.

He picked her up with a strength that surprised her, wrapped her legs around his hips, and pressed her back to the wall. Delphine's stomach tightened in delicious anticipation as Vlad molded their bodies together.

"I think I could get addicted to this," he whispered hotly against her mouth, his crimson pupils pulsing with a fire that threatened to scorch her.

She flashed him a sinful smile, took hold of his face, and claimed his lips.

They never made it to the bedroom.

CHAPTER TWENTY-FIVE

Vlad woke to sunlight warming his face. He blinked groggily.

Memories of last night danced through his mind. His eyes slammed open.

He sat up, hand reaching out blindly for the woman at his side, only to find empty space and cool leather.

His heart sank.

The scent of coffee teased his nostrils. Vlad looked around.

Delphine sat in the window seat overlooking Manhattan. She was wearing his shirt and nothing else, her long legs stretched out in front of her. Steam curled from the mug in her hands as she watched the city below, her expression thoughtful.

Relief clenched Vlad's gut, along with a flood of emotions that made his breath catch.

"You're still here."

She looked over, one eyebrow arching. "Did you think I'd make a run for it?"

"The thought crossed my mind." Vlad relaxed and propped himself on an elbow.

Her gaze danced down his naked chest and lingered on the blanket covering his lower half.

Vlad smiled. "Like what you see?"

Delphine's eyes darkened. "Very much so. I told you I like you, didn't I?"

Heat pooled in Vlad's belly at her words. He rose and crossed the room, conscious of her gaze tracking his movements as he wrapped the blanket around his waist.

"You did." He settled beside her and stole her coffee. "Though I wouldn't mind hearing it again."

Delphine narrowed her eyes. "Don't push your luck."

Vlad laughed and handed her mug back. "Want a fresh cup?"

They ended up curled on the couch and telling each other their life stories.

"Do all super soldiers know how to fight like that?" Vlad twisted a strand of her hair around his finger as she lay in his arms.

"The Immortals trained us." She took a sip of her coffee and rested her head comfortably on his shoulder. "After they rescued us from Greenland, they sent us to foster families all over the world, mostly Immortals, some humans. The older children like Serena were worried it was to isolate us at first. But it didn't take us long to realize that they only wanted us to experience everything we had missed out on and garner a wealth of knowledge and understanding from different cultures and ways of life that would serve us in the future."

"Is that where your accent comes from?" Vlad said curiously.

"Yes." Delphine's expression softened. "I grew up in France. My adoptive family owned a vineyard in Bordeaux."

Vlad watched her face. "You miss them."

"Every day." She smiled faintly. "My grandfather likes to fart the French national anthem at the family Christmas dinner. And I have an uncle who's rescued about twenty dogs." A chuckle left her lips. "My mom is a terrible cook, so much so she is banned from ever hosting our family dinners." Her expression tuned wistful. "I try to see them once a year."

Vlad propped his chin on her head. "How did you guys end up in a mercenary corps together?"

"The Immortals made sure we all met up regularly since we were kids, so we knew one another long before the corps was formed." Her tone grew nostalgic. "After all, those of us who survived the events in Greenland were family, bound by more than just blood. The ones who saved us insisted we should not be stopped from getting to know one another, however much the Immortal Societies feared we might form an alliance and try and take revenge on them."

Vlad sobered at that. Though Serena and Jared had spoken about the Immortals who had spearheaded the daring rescue mission, he still didn't know much about them. Judging from Delphine's words, the super soldiers held them in the highest regard.

"It was Alexa King who suggested Gideon form the corps. He's the smartest one among us."

Vlad startled. "Mila Jackson's mother?"

Delphine stared at him over her shoulder. "You guys met?"

Vlad nodded. "In Philadelphia." He paused. "Did everyone join the corps?"

Delphine shook her head and settled against him again. "Only those who wanted to. We work independently, but we also support the Immortals on critical missions." She put her coffee down, turned until she was lying face down on top of him, and propped her chin on his chest. "What about you? What was it like growing up with Yuliy?"

"It was"—Vlad's mouth curved at the memories—"everything my mother could ever have wished for me. We lived on a grand estate outside St. Petersburg. Gustav and Lena helped Yuliy take care of me when I was growing up. My uncle brought Tarang home when I was six, as an apology for spanking me after I broke my dead mother's favorite hairbrush."

Delphine arched an eyebrow. "The tiger was an apology gift?"

"Yuliy rescued him from a traveling circus." Vlad's expression softened. "No one was more surprised than my uncle when Tarang turned out to be the perfect match for my powers."

Delphine's eyes sparkled. "I can imagine. You suit each other."

She leaned up to kiss him.

Desire licked through Vlad's veins. His hand found her thigh beneath his shirt.

The doorbell rang.

They froze.

"Are you expecting someone?" Delphine said against his lips.

"No."

She frowned and reached for her cell on the coffee table.

Tarang appeared at the top of the stairs, his tail swishing excitedly. He slinked down the steps and disappeared into the foyer as the bell rang again.

Vlad groaned.

The tiger's enthusiasm could only mean one thing.

"Shit."

Delphine showed him the live view from the camera outside. "Is that—?"

"Yup," Vlad said sourly. "That's Mae and Nikolai and their damn familiars."

Delphine slid off him and straightened his shirt where it had ridden up her thighs, her expression growing shuttered.

Vlad took her hand, conscious of what was going through her mind even though she hadn't said a word. "I'm over her."

She chewed her lip. "Are you sure about that?"

Vlad nodded and pulled her in for a quick kiss.

"I realized it the day after we first slept with each other," he murmured against her mouth. "I was already halfway over Mae. You took me over the finish line."

Delphine slowly relaxed. A smile tugged at her lips. "It was a spectacular finish line."

Vlad grinned sultrily and swooped in for another kiss.

There was banging at the door.

"We know you're in there, Vlad!" Mae yelled. "Tarang just told Brim you've been cavorting with your new girlfriend."

A conspiratorial huff issued from the tiger in the foyer.

"It's not even ten a.m.," Nikolai said in a disapproving voice through the door. "Have you no shame?"

Vlad scowled, climbed into his trousers, and stormed over to the entrance. He yanked the door open.

Mae and Nikolai stumbled into the hallway.

"I don't want to hear that from you, asshole!" Vlad hissed at Nikolai.

Tarang greeted them enthusiastically, his tail sweeping the floor with rapid flicks.

Brimstone trotted in and gave the tiger an affectionate head bump.

Mae recovered and beamed. "We brought gifts." She pushed a couple of bags into Vlad's arms and strode past him into the living room. "Now, where's your lady—oh." She stopped at the sight of Delphine. Her expression turned sheepish. "Sorry, we didn't quite realize you were mid-cavort."

"Hi," Delphine said in a quiet voice. "You must be Mae Jin."

The super soldier startled when Mae went over and gave her a quick hug.

"And you are Delphine." Mae stepped back, a warm

smile lighting up her face. "We've heard about you from Lily and Serena."

Nikolai greeted Delphine with a friendly nod, Alastair ruffling his wings on the sorcerer's shoulder.

Delphine had stiffened. "Lily?" Her gaze danced between Mae and Nikolai. "You mean Lily Soul?"

Vlad frowned at the name. "Isn't that the Seer in Chicago? Why would she—?" He froze, the pieces of the puzzle concerning Mae and Nikolai's sudden disappearance finally slotting into place. "Wait," he ground out. "Don't tell me you guys going off grid had something to do with her?!"

"Kinda. We had a situation with the Italian coven, but Lily also told us to make ourselves scarce for a couple of days." Mae scratched her cheek guiltily. "We would have come back if it looked like your plan wasn't going to work. It was the only way to make sure you two—you know." She waggled her eyebrows suggestively.

"We got together?" Delphine's eyes had shrunk to slits.

"I was going to say became friends in the biblical sense, but that works too," Mae said brightly.

Hellreaver quivered on her chest.

"*My witch, my fiends are demanding a sacrifice,*" the demonic weapon rumbled.

Delphine tensed.

"He means he wants meat," Mae told the super soldier hastily as the weapon transformed. She narrowed her eyes at Hellreaver. "And you, how about you stop saying ambiguous things? It's why we got in trouble with those Italians."

Vlad curled a lip. "What'd he do?"

Nikolai shuddered. "You don't wanna know. My leg still aches."

Hellreaver zoomed out of the living room toward the kitchen, Tarang, Brimstone, and Alastair following in his wake.

"Don't make a mess," Mae warned.

"You people know this is my place, right?" Vlad said, incensed.

Nikolai grimaced. "Don't be such a killjoy. Besides, we lived here for a while. Your apartment is practically our second home."

Vlad scowled.

The front door opened. Cortes strode in, Popo on his shoulder. He slowed at the sight of Mae and Nikolai, surprise widening his eyes.

"When did you guys get in town?" he said while Mae greeted him with a kiss on the cheek.

"This morning." Nikolai shook the sorcerer's hand.

Vlad stared at the Colombian. "Since when did you have a key?"

"Since a while back," Cortes said with a nonchalant shrug. He indicated Mae and Nikolai. "They made a copy and gave it to me. I rang the bell the other day because I was being polite."

A headache throbbed at Vlad's temples as he glared at the couple.

"We like it here," Mae said shamelessly. "There's free food, booze, and you have the best entertainment system in Manhattan."

Delphine's mouth twitched. She sobered when Vlad cut his eyes to her. "We should change the locks."

A dirty smile curved Cortes's mouth. "Oh. Are you guys moving in together?"

Popo leaned toward his sorcerer. "It looks like mating conditions were optimal last night, my Enrique," he hissed in a conspiratorial tone.

"I've missed that bird," Nikolai told Mae.

Vlad and Delphine exchanged a hesitant look.

"We haven't broached the subject yet," he said quietly.

Mae wrinkled her nose. "Yeah, you should start packing when you get to Washington," she told Delphine.

Delphine stilled. Vlad lowered his brows suspiciously.

Delphine's cell rang. She checked the screen. "It's Gideon." She took the call and listened for a moment. Her pupils flared. "What?"

"Gideon's gonna give her a job in New York," Mae whispered to Vlad.

Vlad's chest tightened at her smile.

He could tell she was genuinely happy for him.

His gaze switched to Delphine. Though they hadn't discussed the future, the possibility of the super soldier becoming a permanent fixture in New York and in his life was something he very much wanted.

Delphine ended the call.

She met Vlad's stare, her expression a little shocked. "A position just opened up in New York with the Special Affairs Bureau. Gideon wants to assign me as a representative of our corps."

Vlad forced himself to stay still. "What will you do?"

Delphine hesitated. "I—" She stopped and swallowed, her expression growing vulnerable for the first time since he'd met her. "I don't know. It's so sudden."

Vlad closed the distance between them and took her hand, his heart racing.

"Say yes," he breathed, staring into her eyes.

"What?" Delphine blinked. "Are you sure?"

Vlad pressed their lips together in a soft, sweet kiss. "Yes."

Delphine's shoulders unknotted. She smiled tremulously and coiled her arms around his neck. "No take backs."

Vlad grinned and swooped in for another kiss, happiness lightening his heart and body.

"They know we're still here, right?" Nikolai muttered to Mae and Cortes.

THE END

***

Have you read The Party? Join the main protagonists of *Seventeen*, *Legion*, and *Witch Queen* in this delightful short tale full of humor, heart, and a little Christmas magic!

Coming soon!
Diary of A Reluctant Werewolf, or DOARF for short, marks the beginning of a brand new A.D. Starrling series (and hopefully a universe!) full of wacky, unforgettable characters that will have you howling out aloud. The first book, *It All Started With A Bite*, launches spring/summer 2025!

ACKNOWLEDGMENTS

To my friends and family. I couldn't do this without you.

To my readers. Thank you for reading The Incubus and The Bodyguard. If you enjoyed my book, please consider leaving a review on Goodreads or on the store where you purchased it. Reviews help readers like you find my books and I truly appreciate your honest opinions about my stories.

BOOKS BY A.D. STARRLING

Seventeen Novels
Hunted

Warrior

Empire

Legacy

Origins

Destiny

Seventeen Short Stories
First Death

Dancing Blades

The Meeting

The Warrior Monk

The Hunger

The Bank Job

Legion
Blood and Bones

Fire and Earth

Awakening

Forsaken

Hallowed Ground

Heir

Legion

Witch Queen
The Darkest Night
Rites of Passage
Of Flames and Crows
Midnight Witch
A Fury of Shadows
Witch Queen
The Incubus and The Bodyguard

Seventeen Universe
The Party

Division Eight
Mission:Black
Mission: Armor
Mission:Anaconda

Miscellaneous
Void - A Sci-fi Horror Short Story
The Other Side of the Wall - A Horror Short Story

ABOUT A.D. STARRLING

Visit Shop AD Starrling and buy all of AD's ebooks, paperbacks, hardbacks, audiobooks, and exclusive special edition print books direct.

Want to know about AD Starrling's upcoming releases? Sign up to her author newsletter for new release alerts, sneak peeks, giveaways, and more.

Follow AD Starrling on Amazon.

Join AD's reader group on Facebook
The Seventeen Club.

Check out this link to find out more about A.D. Starrling Linktr.ee/AD_Starrling.